autumn's kiss

autumn's kiss

BELLA THORNE

with **ELISE ALLEN**

SCHOLASTIC INC.

ISBN 978-1-338-13907-5

12 11 10 9 8 7 6 5 4 3 2 1   16 17 18 19 20 21

Printed in the U.S.A.   40

This edition first printing, September 2016

1

♥♥♥♥♥♥

"Let's go!" I holler. I've already been hollering for two hours, so my voice rasps in my throat. I'm sweating buckets even though I'm wearing a tank and shorts—in the beginning of October—but I'm used to that now. That's how life is in Aventura, Florida. We sweat until the thunderstorms shower us clean, and then we sweat again. "Go, Indians!"

"No Indians!" Even though she's right next to me, my friend Reenzie has to shout so I'll hear her over the crowd. "Remember?"

"Reenzie, come on," I whine. "It's the team's name!"

"It's offensive to Native Americans!" she shoots back. "I have the whole online petition."

"You're only doing that to look good on college applications," I remind her. Then the crowd noise rises a million decibels and we both whip our faces toward the field. A guy in tight turquoise pants is running really, really fast and keeps ducking out of the way of guys in tight black pants.

"YES!" I shout as if I have any clue what's going on. "YES! GO!"

The ever-increasing roar from the crowd tells me cheering was the right choice. I keep screaming as the turquoise guy runs all the way to the part of the field with our team's name on it. Even I know what that means.

"Touchdown!" All my friends and I scream it together, and Reenzie and I are so excited, we throw our arms around each other and jump up and down, but Reenzie pulls away to yell at our friends J.J. and Jack for doing a bad version of a Native American tribal dance.

"Offensive!" she shouts, pointing at them.

"Reenzie, half the stadium's doing it," I tell her. "You've got to let it go." Then I lean past the guys to yell over the noise, "Tee, you have the popcorn?"

Taylor nods, then scoots past J.J. and Jack so she can hand me the bucket and she, Reenzie, and I can share it. She leans down to my much-lower-than-hers head and points to a guy three rows in front of us and a little off to the side. "There's your boyfriend."

I do a spit-take on the popcorn. The guy has to be at least fifty—we get a lot of alums at Aventura High games—and there's nacho sauce threaded through his way-too-bushy-for-this-kind-of-humidity beard.

"Spew *away* from the bucket," Reenzie tells me, but I'm already scanning the stands for a worthy comeback. Then I hear the loud dual stomp that means we're about to start another football ritual.

For my fans,

for all of their support

through the years

"DE-FENSE!" *Stomp-stomp.* "DE-FENSE!" *Stomp-stomp.*

I join in. I have no idea what I'm rooting for, but it's our side of the stadium that's saying it, so it's a safe bet it's something good. Plus, our cheerleaders are shouting along. I find my friend Amalita among them. She's the shortest and probably the roundest, but she out-handsprings every beanpole on the squad. I mimic her hand motions as I keep up the cheer.

The whole stadium—or at least the home team side—thrums and echoes with our stomps and shouts. I feel like I'm part of something huge, like I'm having a wild out-of-body experience I'm sharing with everyone else here.

High school football is the greatest sport in the world.

I never realized it when I lived in Maryland, because there, it wasn't. Here, it's huge. Plus, now I understand how it works.

Here's the deal. It starts Friday at school, when everyone competes to see how many items of clothing in the school colors you can pile onto your body. Granted, our school colors are turquoise and purple—not a combo I'd advise under any other circumstance—but on game day it works. Accessories count, as does face paint.

So I guess that would be the first quarter of the football game—the Fashion Pile-On. Then there's the pep rally right after school. Pep rallies back in Maryland? Lame and not cool. Here it's a Thing, and I'm all about Things. Everyone goes, and the goal is to scream your throat rawer than anyone else's. That's like the second quarter—the

Shriek-Off. The third quarter involves speed: You scoot home, change out of your old set of school-color clothes and into a fresh one, grab whatever snacks you can mash into a cooler, then meet your friends at a prearranged location with plenty of time to get to the stadium and find seats before the game. The details are essential here. You need to achieve the maximum level of cute in the minimum amount of time, because the bleachers fill up fast. Extra points for bringing the best snacks, penalties for not arriving with a big enough group of friends. Four is the minimum acceptable.

The fourth quarter is the pregame show, meaning our school taunts the visitors on the other side of the stadium. Lots of bleacher pounding, more screaming, and the challenge of not scarfing all the snacks before the game starts. When the band comes onto the field, that signals the end of the fourth quarter: time to tune out and take selfies while they play the school song, then scream like crazy when the guy on the PA announces our players. We cheer as if they're rock stars like Kyler Leeds, even if they're just the jerks who made gross mouth noises during the last school assembly. That's how psyched we are.

Fifth quarter? The game. Time to figure out which players look good in their football tights and which you'd rather not see, take selfies in the stands and post on Instagram, play "there's your boyfriend" while pointing at the least likely candidates, finish the snacks everyone brought and cave on the overpriced school-sponsored popcorn and nachos, and either scream to your friends over the stadium noise or, if something's a secret, scramble around in your row so you can get to someone's ear.

Oh yeah—and whenever the guy on the PA sounds really excited, you know it's time to look at the field. If one of our guys is catching something from super far away, kicking something through the goalposts, or running into the area where the team's name is painted on the grass, we get to make as much noise as humanly possible.

Finally, there's going out afterward. You get greasy, sugary food, and everyone sounds like they're in a wind tunnel because your ears are fried from all the screaming. It's like you're floating on a cloud of awesome. It doesn't even matter if the team won or lost, except you got to scream more if they won, so that's a little more fun. The afterthing would be the sixth quarter, I guess.

Is that too many quarters? I'm really bad at math.

I hear another roar from the crowd.

"Touchdown!" I squeal, only this time I'm squealing alone.

J.J. leans over Taylor. "*Their* touchdown," he informs me. "The tights of blue belong to you."

He's teasing me, telling me I need a sad excuse of a rhyme to remember which team is ours. "Oh, please, like you never made a mistake like that. Did you even go to football games before I got here?"

J.J. and Taylor swap places so he and I can keep talking without screaming. "Are you trying to say your arrival on the scene changed my life?"

"Changed it for the *better*."

Reenzie grabs my arm in a vise grip and points at the field. "Autumn! It's Sean! They did a flea flicker but he had no viable receivers! He's running with it!"

Allow me to translate that to Autumn-Falls-ese:

"Autumn! It's Sean! Warble-blurble-static-noise-flumfle . . . running!"

Running? Sean? In those tights?

I turn and watch.

I wish I could say it's one of those moments when time slows and I can just soak up his every move as he bounds down the field, but it doesn't work that way. If I wanted the slo-mo, I'd have to watch the game footage and play it back that way, and that would just be creepy. Besides, even though Sean looks good on the field, his helmet hides his best feature—those blue eyes that make me think of crisp ponds, clear waterfalls, and running my hands over his perfectly toned biceps as he reaches for the back of my head and pulls me close. . . .

Whoa, that got a little out of hand, especially since Sean and I are so not there. Not anymore. Not that we *were*. I mean, we *kind of* were. We were kissing. Just not in that climax-of-a-Gothic-romance way I'd just imagined. And that was before I did some stupid things . . . to get back at

Reenzie for doing some *evil* things . . . which it turned out she mainly did because she wanted Sean and was jealous. But after it all went down, he didn't want to be with either one of us and it all got gross and complicated and I was convinced no one in the state except my mom, my brother, my grandmother, and *maybe* J.J. and Amalita would ever talk to me again.

But then I did something nice for Taylor. And since she's friends with both the Sean/Reenzie/Zach group and the Amalita/J.J./Jack group, she amazingly, miraculously managed to bring us all together.

If she didn't look like a Barbie doll, I'd think she was a witch.

Or maybe she looks like a Barbie doll *because* she's a witch.

"Ooooh," the crowd moans as a pack of guys throw themselves on Sean. The last one on the pile has to be two hundred pounds. How does Sean breathe under all that?

"Hey, Tee," Reenzie calls, and Taylor again swaps places with J.J. so she's right next to me. "There's your boyfriend."

Reenzie points to a guy moving our way up the stairs. He's scuttling quickly, like he was talking to someone in a lower bleacher and is now going back to his own seat. Despite the insane heat and humidity, he's wearing a white button-down with the sleeves rolled up. At least he's in shorts. They're red and stretch down to his knees. His mop of brown hair bounces playfully as he runs.

Taylor lights up. She waves her arms. "Ryan! *Ryan!*"

Ryan looks over and glows just as much when he sees her. He stretches out his arms. "Sarah, darling!" he squeals.

"Sky, my love!" she cries. She pushes her way past Reenzie and me so she can throw her arms around him. He's a couple inches taller than her, and the two of them rock back and forth as they hug. When they pull apart, Ryan keeps his hands on her shoulders and looks her right in the eye like there's no one else in the world.

"Are you loving this?" he asks, and I'm not sure if he's talking about the musical they were just reenacting or the crazy-exciting atmosphere around us. But it doesn't matter to Taylor—she loves anything Ryan does.

"Beyond—so fun!"

"I know! Next week we should sit together, okay?"

"I'd love that!"

"Call me tonight," he says. "We can run lines."

"Yes!"

"Done." He pulls her in again and kisses her on the cheek; then, as he races up the stairs, he sings, *"I've never been in love before . . . now all at once it's you . . . it's you forever more . . ."*

It's a song from *Guys and Dolls*. It's the fall musical, and Taylor plays one of the female leads. Ryan plays her boyfriend in the show, and she's dying for him to take on the same role in real life. After he leaves, she floats back to her seat.

"Gay," Reenzie says.

"Shut up!" Taylor snaps.

"I'm not saying it's bad," Reenzie says. "Just that it's a fact."

"Not every actor is gay," Taylor says.

"Not actor—high school musical theater guy," Reenzie clarifies.

"Not every high school musical theater guy is gay!" Taylor maintains. "*Kyler Leeds* definitely isn't, and I read that he practically grew up in musical theater."

Kyler Leeds happens to be my own personal obsession, but Taylor and Amalita got to hang out with him last spring for a "Night of Dreams." They sang karaoke that night, and apparently Kyler told Taylor she was so good she should try out for musicals. The rest is history.

"Kyler Leeds is *totally* gay," J.J. says.

"Shut up!" I say.

"How about Ryan Darby?" Reenzie leans forward to ask the guys.

"Gay," J.J. replies, and Jack immediately adds, "Oh yeah. Without question."

Taylor sits back in her seat, looking miffed. "I hate you all, and none of you are invited to my and Ryan's wedding."

An air horn blows. The crowd erupts. I look for the scoreboard, but everyone is on their feet and I can't see it.

"What happened? Did we score?"

"It's over!" Jack shouts. "We won!"

"WE WOOOOOON!" I screech. I hoot and howl and jump up and down, and this time when the band comes out on the field and plays the school song, we all sing along.

"Soft serve?" Taylor asks. She already has her phone out, ready to text Ames so she can meet us wherever we go once she changes out of her uniform and does whatever bizarre postgame rituals cheerleaders do. Jack assumes it has something to do with human sacrifice, but Jack's weird.

"Shack at Deerfield Beach," Reenzie says, already texting it. "I'm telling Sean."

For just an instant, I want to lunge at Reenzie and breathe fire, but then I get it under control. The jealous thing is crazy. Sean and Reenzie are *not* a couple. Sean made it crystal clear after everything went down last spring that even though he had feelings for both of us, he was also pretty disgusted by us both and only wanted to be friends. And, yes, Reenzie is as hopeful as I am—if not more—that he'll change his mind and go from *our* friend to *her* boyfriend. And sure, she's known him forever, knows every detail about his life, including all the little things he loves best, and she looks like a Victoria's Secret model, so the odds seem stacked in her favor. But I know I'm the one with the upper hand. While Sean was away from town all summer driving around with his older brothers and hitting college football camps, he texted me almost every day. I have the pictures on my phone to prove it, shots of him with bizarre landmarks from all over the country: him grinning with the statue of the Jolly Green Giant in Minnesota; cuddling next to a statue of a giant sock monkey in Illinois; pretending to throw a stick for the Dog Park Bark Inn—an Idaho bed-and-breakfast shaped like a giant beagle . . .

Stuff like that. Stuff he knew I'd appreciate and think was funny. Stuff that showed he was thinking about me the whole time. And, no, when he got home, he didn't race to my house, sweep me into his arms, and kiss me—not that I had that fantasy . . . more than once an hour—but he's always smiley and a little flirty and we still text and joke all the time and . . .

It'll happen is what I'm saying. Sean and I will happen. I just have to be patient and keep reminding myself that no matter how Reenzie makes it seem, I'm the one he's moving toward, not her. It's *my* name that's written in the grass of his end zone.

Or something like that.

2

We're out of the stadium now, and I dance-walk as we make our way to the parking lot. It's a very Amalita thing to do, but I'm on a high from the game and every car around is blaring their radios crazy loud out the open windows and shouting and honking at anyone wearing Aventura High colors. We "WHOOO!" back at each one. With the sun down, I can even pretend it's cool outside, though it's actually still at least eighty degrees out and so humid I'm ready to leap into any body of cool liquid. A cup of orange juice, that would be fine. I'd dive right in.

Taylor joins me in the walking boogie. We bump hips every other step, even though she has to squat down so her hip doesn't nail me in the waist.

"Repeat after me," J.J. tells me between hip bumps. "Shotgun."

I take his hand and lift it so I can spin underneath. I've seen him dance—not with me, but with his on-again/off-again girlfriend Carrie Amernick—and I know he's good, but letting it out in a parking lot isn't his thing. Moving him is like moving a long, lean plank. Still, it's not like he stiffens up more or pulls away, so I do what he asks.

"Shotgun!"

"Winner!" J.J. cries. "Autumn Falls gets to ride right up front in Earl!"

"Real men name their cars after women," Jack says.

"Real men don't keep their *Star Wars* Legos," J.J. shoots back.

"It's an X-wing fighter," Jack says. "Vintage 1999, the first year for official *Star Wars* Legos. Plus, it comes with Luke Skywalker, Biggs Darklighter, *and* a Rebel technician."

"You do know you're talking out loud, right?" Taylor asks. "We can all hear you."

"Especially me," Reenzie sneers. "And you just lost riding privileges in my car."

"Ergo," J.J. declares to Jack, "you're in the back of Earl. Earl Yimmidy. Which is an anagram of?"

"My daily ride," I say.

I know it because I came up with it. At least, I came up with the *my daily ride* part. J.J. figured out the anagram. Anagrams are J.J.'s thing. He's a freak for them.

"Branching off, Tee." Reenzie rolls her eyes. "These people are weird."

She and Taylor peel off toward Reenzie's car while the rest of us keep walking to J.J.'s. Even though we all drove in at the same time, J.J. insisted we park an eternity away so he didn't have to park Earl Yimmidy next to any other vehicle that might dent it in any possible way. He's a little insane about the new car.

"Are your hands clean?" J.J. asks as I reach for the passenger-side door.

"Shut up," I reply.

The car *is* nice. Cars aren't my thing, so I know absolutely zero about it, even though J.J. has given me the full rundown about a zillion times and even offered to lend me the manual in case I needed some reading material.

Like I would (A) ever need reading material—I'm dyslexic, which J.J. knows, and the stuff I have to read for school is more than enough—or (B) ever in an eternity dream of reading a *car manual* for fun.

What I know about his car is the important stuff: it's sleek, it's black, I can adjust the passenger seat so it's completely comfortable, and as long as I take off my shoes and use one of J.J.'s car wipies before I get out, he lets me lean back and put my feet up on the dashboard, which is what I do now . . . after I choose one of the Sirius XM radio stations J.J. let me preset.

"Hey, Autumn." Jack leans forward from the backseat. "When are you getting your license?"

"This time next never," I shoot back lightly.

"Why not?" he asks. "Everyone wants to drive. It's un-American to be in high school and not want to drive."

"I don't need to drive," I say. I hear my voice getting a

little tighter, but I try not to let it show. "You guys all drive, my mom drives, I can take the bus. . . ."

"What about after graduation?" Jack persists.

"What if I go to NYU?" I snap back, wheeling to face him. "No one drives in New York, right?"

"What if you go to FSU?" he asks. "Everyone drives in Florida . . . except you."

"At least Autumn would get into FSU," J.J. says. "How'd that PSAT go for you?"

Jack's face goes bright red. We only took the PSATs last week and won't know our scores until December, but Jack's pretty sure he completely bombed it. I don't even know that firsthand. He told J.J. in confidence because he was totally freaked out, and I know he's got to be furious and mortified that J.J.'s talking about it in front of me. Normally, J.J. wouldn't. I mean, yeah, he'd tell me because we kind of tell each other just about everything, but he wouldn't bring it up in front of Jack. He's doing it on purpose because he knows the real reason I won't drive, and he knows I don't want to talk about it, so he had to do something big to shut Jack up.

I meet J.J.'s eyes and smile so he knows I get it. He smirks back at me. Say what you will about my lanky friend J.J. with the skin as vampire-pale as my own, but he has a great smirk. I enjoy it for a second, then lean forward and turn up the music so we can all stop seething and just rock out.

Deerfield Beach isn't far, and when we're almost there, I say to J.J., "Hit it."

15

We've done this enough that he knows what I mean. He turns off the A/C, rolls down the windows, and opens the sunroof. It's basically a cardinal sin to turn off the A/C in Florida, but near the beach it's okay. The air here actually feels a little cool, and it smells thick and salty. I lean my head out and take deep breaths. With my orange hair flapping in my face, I probably look like a giant Irish setter, but I don't care.

We park in the lot of an old motel right on the beach. Half the school goes to the Shack for ice cream after Friday night football games and its parking lot is insanely jammed, but the motel is always so empty I don't know how it stays in business. Plus, there's no fence or anything, so we can just pull right in and walk to the Shack—it's all of a minute away.

Reenzie and Taylor are already waiting for us, sitting on the hood of Reenzie's car, but they jump off and run over when they see us. Taylor throws open my door. "So what do you think?"

"About what?"

"The tiger suit!" Taylor cries. "Didn't you see it? I texted you!"

I didn't hear my phone in the car, but I pull it out now. She sent me a picture of a woman with an absolutely perfect body slipped into a fuzzy orange-brown sheath with black stripes and a sheer white circle—the tiger's stomach—that shows off half her boobs.

"Are you kidding me?" I wail.

"You don't see it?" Taylor asks. "With your red hair? This would look incredible on you!"

We're walking toward the Shack now, and I tuck my phone in my back pocket. "No way," I say. "I don't have the body to pull that off."

"That's what Reenzie said," Taylor admits, "but I think it would look really cute."

I glare openmouthed at Reenzie. *Really?*

"What?" she says. "I'm being honest. I'm not saying you have a *bad* body, just that it takes a very specific shape to pull that off well."

"Pull what off well?" J.J. asks.

"Nothing," Reenzie, Taylor, and I chorus.

"Come on, let us see," Jack says.

"No!" I say.

"It's not like you're *in* it," Jack says. Then he leers. "Are you?"

"NO!"

"Look, it's just this," Taylor says. She hands Jack her own phone, which I guess has the costume on it.

Jack grins. "I like it."

"Of course you do, perv," I say. Sometimes Jack reminds me of my little brother, Erick, which makes me fear for Erick's future.

"Now picture Autumn in it," Reenzie says pointedly.

"*No. Stop,*" I insist. "Do *not* picture Autumn in it."

"Picture Autumn in what?"

My heart stops at Sean's voice. If we're not together—or

once we've been hanging out for like an hour or so and I'm used to it—I can be more patient and totally handle the just-friends thing. But whenever I first see him, this happens. My whole body gets flushed and my heart pounds and every single time he's touched or kissed me flashes through my head like I'm living it all over again.

I'm almost afraid to meet his eyes, like he'll see inside me and know exactly what I'm thinking. At the same time I *want* him to see it. Maybe if he understood how I feel, he'd finally get completely over everything that happened and we could be together again.

I lift my eyes to his, and I'm immediately sucked in. He's in long shorts and a school T-shirt, and his dark skin practically glows in the moonlight. His hair is still wet from the shower, and most of it is combed back from his forehead, but one wisp is sticking up. I'm dying to reach out and smooth it down . . . maybe lingering with my hands on his shoulders . . . staring into his eyes . . .

"Hey!" Reenzie chirps. "How did you get here before us?"

She prances into his arms like she belongs there, gives him a huge hug, then pauses in his arms to smooth the wayward chunk of hair.

I want to whip out my phone and show her all the pictures he sent me on his summer trip. Then she'd know who he thinks about when he's away and she'd back off. Or she wouldn't back off—she can get away with hanging on him like they're a couple even when they're not because Sean says she's like his sister. For the record, I would never in a million years crawl on Erick that way, even if he did look like Sean. In fact, ew.

"Got a ride from McNack," Sean says. "He dropped a bunch of us off so we didn't have to park and walk. You guys like the game?"

I'm still not happy about Reenzie diving into Sean's arms, but since the upshot is that the conversation moves away from me in the tiger suit, I can be okay with it. While we all talk about the game and stand in line for ice cream, I snag Taylor's phone out of Jack's hands and give it back to her.

"You *do* need a costume, though," she whispers to me. "Reenzie's party's only a week away."

"I know," I say. "I'll figure something out."

I say it, even though actually doing it sounds like torture. I'm not supposed to figure out my own Halloween costume. I'm not supposed to be free Halloween night. I'm supposed to be at my own ridiculously tricked-out house, having my own major party with my friends, Erick's friends, and my parents' friends, and my outfit is supposed to be a whole-family coordinated adventure—something dorky yet amazing that my dad started planning and my mom started creating May 31, which is Halloween's half-birthday.

My dad was seriously into Halloween. It was his favorite holiday.

We're next in line for ice cream when a van pulls up

and a slew of squealing, bouncing, and somersaulting girls pile out. The cheerleaders. They do a quick "GO INDIANS!" and then split off in a million directions like breaking pool balls.

"*¡Mis amigos!*" Amalita throws her arms in the air and runs toward us. "Did you see I did an aerial? Did you see it? When I jumped off the pyramid!"

We all tell her we did and it was amazing. Some of us might have actually seen it happen too.

"What about you?" She smacks Sean's arm. "You didn't see?"

"I was playing football!" Sean protests.

"Make it up to me," Ames insists. "Point me to Denny."

Sean points to the road. "I tried to convince him to stay. He's hard-core."

"*¡Que verracos pasa!*" Amalita groans. "He never goes anywhere!"

"Except to the gateway of your heart," Taylor sighs, purposely sounding like a Disney princess.

"*Callate*, Tay," Ames says. "This boy is making me *loco*."

"I was watching him today," I say. Denny McNack was one of the guys on the field who *definitely* pulled off the turquoise tights. "He's cute."

Sean scrunches his brows and shoots me a look. Does he not like that I noticed another guy?

"*Really* cute." I lay it on. "Did you get to hang with him at all during the game?"

"No!" Ames gripes. We stop the conversation so we can

order and get our cones; then she keeps going. "I never hang with him at all. He knows who I am—he winks at me every time he passes me, and he doesn't do that to any of the other cheerleaders. I asked. But if he's not on the field, he's always talking to his stupid coach or quarterback or wearing his headphones and riding the exercise bike—like he's not exercising by running up and down the court."

"Field," Sean corrects her. "And *I'm* the stupid quarterback. And the bike's to keep him warm when the defense is on the field."

"So if it's so important, how come you're not on the bike?" Ames asked.

"I ride it sometimes," Sean says defensively. "But he's a running back. He's the fastest guy on the team. He has to be. He's the main reason we've only lost one game."

"I'm sure you have a lot to do with it too," Reenzie says, putting her hand on Sean's cut bicep.

It's such a kiss-up move. I'm totally annoyed she did it before I could.

Sean rewards her with a humbly adorable smile. "Thanks. But Denny's a senior and he's seriously pro-level amazing. He did the whole summer football college camp thing like I did, and *every* school tried to recruit him. Some guy with the Patriots already reached out to him, even though Denny won't even be pro eligible for four years."

"This is all noise," Ames says. "It has nothing to do with me."

"It does," J.J. assures her. "He's saying Denny's not

available for you because he's all about getting ready for college, followed by a career in professional football . . ."

". . . followed by early-onset Alzheimer's from too many concussions," Jack finishes.

Sean's jaw clenches. He likes J.J., but Jack wasn't his favorite addition to his circle of friends. Sean was too nice to say anything, but I have a feeling that at times like this, he wishes his beefy bodyguard of a friend Zach hadn't moved away over the summer.

"Hey!" I shout, breaking the tension. "Race you all to the water!"

I'm finished with my cone, so I kick off my flip-flops and run across the grassy patch in front of the Shack and down the long sandy swath of beach to the ocean. I'm at the edge of the waves for literally one second before two strong arms wrap around my waist and I'm hoisted into the air. I scream, then look down and see Sean's face smiling up at me as he keeps running.

"What are you doing?" I squeal.

"Too much momentum," he says. "It was pick you up or tackle you."

Tackle me! I want to say . . . but I don't. He slows down and places me back on the sand just as everyone else catches up with us. For the next hour we just hang out. We splash through the warm ocean water up to our ankles, we write stupid things in the wet sand and let the waves wash them away, we lie in the sand and look up at the moon and just talk and laugh. I'm doing that at one point, lying back and grinning at the list of anagrams J.J.'s making for "Taylor Darby" ("Adorably Try," "Broadly Arty," "Dry Altar Boy"). Then I rise up on my elbows and just look out at the ocean. The waves roll in, one after the other, and the moon shines off them, and all I can hear are the voices and laughter of my friends.

I take a deep breath, and in that moment I feel more alive than I ever have.

It makes me really happy for about a second . . . until I think about the flip side, and the person who *isn't* alive anymore.

My dad thought I had a mission in life, to bring peace and happiness to my little corner of the world. I spent a lot of time thinking about that when I first moved to Aventura, and a lot of time messing it up. At a certain point I thought I figured it out. I made some choices and brought people together . . . and I kind of thought I'd succeeded. I mean, here I am, in a place I came to kicking and screaming less than a year ago, and now I'm surrounded by friends I really care about. Things *are* peaceful and harmonious.

But I wonder . . . would my dad really want me to just sit back and stop? Maybe I should be doing more. Maybe things could be . . . more peaceful. More harmonious.

I look at Taylor. She's flat on her back, hands over her face, trying not to laugh as everyone pelts her with their vision of her Big Gay Wedding to Ryan Darby. It's funny, but honestly, he could just as easily be straight. And if it would make Taylor happy to go out with him, why shouldn't I make that happen?

Then I look at Amalita. She's laughing with everyone else, but at the same time she's using a shell to carve *A.L. + D.M.* inside a heart in the sand.

Ames is a catch. And if Denny's already flirting with her, he'd probably only need a little push to actually find time to ask her out.

I look at Reenzie next. She's looking at Sean so dreamily I can practically see the cartoon hearts in her eyes.

Sorry, can't help you there. Reenzie and I might be friends now, but I'm not a masochist.

Taylor and Ames, though? They're a task worth taking on. I promise myself that the minute I get home I'm going to do something I haven't done in ages.

I'm going to write in my journal.

3

I turn the key in the door gently. It's late, and Mom works at her rescue shelter, Catches Falls, early Saturday mornings, so I know there's a good chance she's asleep.

I shouldn't have bothered. First I trip over our basset hound, Schmidt, who's lying *right* in front of the door. I slap/clunk down to my hands and knees, but my fall is completely drowned out by the wild gunfight coming from our family room. I walk in to find my twelve-year-old brother, Erick, and one of his buddies standing on the couch and screaming as they play on the Wii. The TV screen is a gruesome mess of body parts, blood, and zombies, which is almost as gross as the fact that both Erick and his friend are wearing hideous rubber monster masks for no possible reason on earth.

Erick is the taller of the beasts, which I realize when his voice roars gleefully out of the snaggle-toothed mask. "It's after midnight! You're gonna be in major trouble!"

"So not," I tell him. "I called Mom and told her. She said it was okay. And by the way, none of your business."

The smaller creature pulls off his mask to reveal Erick's best friend, Aaron. His face is bright red and covered in sweat. "Hi, Autumn," he says. "Did Erick tell you I'm taking guitar lessons?"

Why would he? "Nope. You sleeping over?"

Aaron grins, and his already red face turns even redder. "Yup."

I choke down a gag as I realize he's acting like he has a crush on me. Ignore . . . ignore and hope I'm wrong.

"Don't stay up all night," I say. "G'night."

"Night, Autumn," Erick says, while Aaron chirps, "See you in the morning!"

Whatever. I grab a late-night Diet Coke and take it up to my room. Once I'm in my pajamas, I sit on my bed and look up at my bookcase. The journal's there, on the top shelf, and part of me thinks it's crazy that I don't just grab it and write in it . . . but it's been months. And it's not just a journal. It's my dad.

I know, that sounds ridiculous and even crazy, and believe me, I'm not saying my dad is physically *in* the journal. It's not some Tom Riddle/horcrux thing. I don't know *what* it is exactly. . . . I only know that somehow the journal is tied to my dad's spirit, and when I write in it and say, *I wish* for something . . . the wish sometimes comes true. Not in the way that if you wish on a penny and throw it in a fountain it sometimes coincidentally comes true, but in the way that the journal actually *makes* things I wish for come true.

Sometimes. When it wants to. Even when I don't want it to do exactly what it does. *Obstinado,* that's what my grandmother Eddy calls it. My dad left the journal with her and told her to give it to me so I could use it to bring peace and harmony to my little corner of the world. Which I did. And which I want to do again . . . only I know I need to be careful, because while the journal did some great things for me last year, it also messed things up pretty terribly. That's why I stopped writing in it.

Actually, that's not fair. It wasn't the journal that messed things up. *I* did. The journal was just listening to me.

So maybe it'll be okay if I try writing in it again. I'll just be more careful.

I reach up and pull down the journal. The familiar feel of the leather makes me all warm inside, and I'm amazed I let it sit for so long. I look at the cover, eager to see the familiar three-point *zemi:* the triangle with what looks like a face in it, the symbol that my dad's people, the Taino, believed held the spirits of their dead ancestors.

I guess I believe that too . . . except the symbol isn't there. The front cover of the book is plain milk-chocolate brown.

That's impossible. I must be holding the book the wrong way. I flip it over . . . but the other side is as blank as the front.

Did the symbol wear away?

Impossible. It was etched into the leather. I remember running my fingers over it and feeling its deep grooves. That kind of thing doesn't wear out. It's part of the leather forever.

Just in case, I carefully feel every inch of the cover, front and back. If the embossed symbol *did* somehow get shallower and harder to see, I should still be able to feel it, if only a little.

Nothing. The cover feels perfectly smooth, without a single imperfection.

Fury rises inside me as I realize the only possible answer, and I can't believe I didn't think of it right away.

This isn't my journal. When I was away this summer working as a camp-counselor-in-training with Jenna, my best friend from home, Erick must have raided my room, even though I made him swear he wouldn't set foot in it. He was probably *looking* for a diary so he and his stupid friends could read it. Then he must have ruined it or something—or even worse, *kept* the thing—and found a near look-alike to try and replace it so I wouldn't know.

I get a hideous image in my head of Erick and Aaron in their monster masks jumping on the couch and reading parts of my journal out loud to one another. My stomach churns. I feel even more nauseous when I think about the actual things he read—not just me talking directly to Dad as if he were in the journal, but every nightmarish thing that happened to me last year—stuff I would rather die than have Erick know.

I'm going to kill him. That's the only answer.

I storm downstairs, journal in my hand, but something stops me and I look again at the book.

I pull it open and read.

Dear Dad,

I know you're not connected to this thing, and it's not like you can actually read it . . .

It's my writing. My entry. I flip through and see every entry I wrote.

It's all there. This is my journal. If Erick took it, he put it back with a new cover. Would he have done that, maybe? If he somehow ruined the old cover?

No. He couldn't. It's a bound book. It would be next to impossible to rebind a bound book—he'd have to have it done professionally. And honestly, if he'd had the time and money to do it, he'd have made sure a matching *zemi* was on the new cover.

I slowly walk back to my room. Erick will live another day, but I still don't understand. If this is my journal, where is the *zemi*?

I want to call Jenna, but it's way after midnight by now. Saturday mornings are her long run days, so I know she's been asleep for hours. I grab my phone and take a picture of the blank front and back covers and text them to her anyway. I also explain everything. She's the only person who knows everything about the journal, so I know she'll have advice.

I flop down on my bed and stare at the cover.

No *zemi*.

Nothing holding the spirits of dead ancestors.

Does that mean no Dad? Is it just a regular journal now? One way to find out.

I roll over and grab a pen, then flip to the first blank page.

Dear Dad . . .

I'll make this short because I'm not positive you're there anymore . . .

I'm surprised to feel tears springing to my eyes. I blink them away and keep writing.

I wish that tomorrow morning . . .

I need something good. Something not so obvious that it would happen anyway and therefore proves nothing, but not something so outrageous that the journal will get stubborn and not want to do it.

It hurts when I hit on the right answer. It's something I secretly want badly, and something that *could* happen, but I haven't seen any sign of it yet.

I wish that when I wake up tomorrow and see Mom, she'll tell me she's come up with costumes for her,

Erick, and me, and that we'll decorate the house for Halloween and have our regular party like always.

I know for me it'll be a pretty lame party, since all my friends are already committed to Reenzie's. I probably can't even invite them without getting her upset since hers came first. But that's okay. I don't care if anyone's there for me or not. I just want to have Dad's favorite holiday the way he liked it.

Tears fall on the page, and I dab them away so they don't smear what I just wrote. I close the journal and sleep with it under my pillow.

I don't wake up until after noon. When I check my phone, there's a message from Jenna:

Show journal to Eddy! Then call and tell me what she said. Miss you! P.S. Glad you didn't kill Erick. Sorta.

I laugh out loud. Erick has had a mad crush on Jenna forever. She tolerates it, but it grosses us both out.

She's probably right. I should bring the journal to Eddy. But Jenna doesn't know about the wish I made after I texted her. I pull the journal from under my pillow and read it again, just so I can remember exactly how I asked; then I put it back and head downstairs. The house smells like cookies.

"Mom!" I say when I see her bustling around the kitchen. She's wearing yoga pants and a tank top, and her long dark curls are piled on her head in a loose bun. "I thought you were at Catches Falls today."

"I was supposed to be, but the boys stayed up all night, so they're still out, and I didn't want to just leave them without asking if you were okay watching them."

"I'm sorry," I say, flopping into a kitchen chair. "You could have gotten me up. I'd have been fine with it."

Mom smiles, then kisses the top of my head. She can only do that when I'm sitting, because I'm taller than her, which never ceases to be a little weird.

"It's okay," she says. "I had one of the girls go in instead. Besides, I wanted to be home today. I want to talk to you about Halloween."

I feel a flutter over my skin. Halloween? Is this about my wish?

"Pumpkin muffin?" she asks.

That explains the cookie smell. I nod, and Mom butters one for me while I try to be patient and not jump in and ask her what she wants to say about Halloween. Then I notice she has a photo album out on the counter. I walk over to it. It's open to a full-page picture from last year: Mom, Dad, Erick, and I standing in front of the house in Maryland. It's nighttime, and the house is a wild mix of spiderwebs, tombstones, skeletons, and eerie lights. I remember there was a smoke machine too, but you can't tell in the picture. And Dad had rigged the doorbell so it shrieked when anyone pressed it. We're dressed as the characters from *The Nightmare Before Christmas*. Erick is Jack, I'm Sally, Dad is Oogie Boogie, Mom's the mayor of Halloween Town, and Schmidt's Zero. As I flip backward in the album, I see us in the same place, growing younger page after page, each time with a new theme. On one page we're the Addams Family; on one we're traditional monsters—Frankenstein, the Wolfman, Dracula, and a mummy; on one we're Freddy Krueger, Jason, the Tall Man, and Leatherface; on one we're Fred, Velma, Daphne, and Shaggy. In that one, Schmidt is Scooby-Doo. The album goes all the way back to Mom and Dad outside a college party, dressed up as a ghost couple from Disney's Haunted Mansion, with their clothes and entire bodies all made the same shade of powder-white.

I don't even realize Mom's looking over my shoulder until she laughs. "You have no idea how long it took me to get that white stuff out of our hair. My first idea was even worse. I tried using flour, thinking it would look good and powdery, but when I washed *that* out, it clumped and clogged up the only good shower on my dorm room floor. I have friends who still give me a hard time about it."

"It was fun," I say, "dressing up together."

"Yeah, it was."

Mom puts her arm around me and steers me back to the table, where she's laid out the muffin and a cup of chamomile tea for each of us. As we sit, she adds, "But I'm glad you have Reenzie's party to go to this year."

"You are?"

"Mmm-hmm. I was worried about Erick, but last night Aaron invited him to spend Halloween at his house, trick-or-treat, then spend the night. Now, I figure you're going to be at that party pretty late. . . . Do you think you'd be able to stay overnight? If not at Reenzie's house, maybe Amalita's or Taylor's?"

"Why?"

Mom grins. "My friend Amanda found a deal online at a hotel in Miami. Spa treatments, room service, a beautiful pool . . . We want to get there before dinner and make a whole night of it, come home the next afternoon."

"You're not going to be here giving out candy?"

Mom suddenly looks exhausted. "I'm not up for it." She opens her mouth like she's going to say more, then shakes her head. "I'd rather just go away and pretend it's not Halloween at all. You don't mind, do you? You don't even have to stay away overnight—I just thought if you didn't want to be here alone, and you'd be out so late with your friends anyway . . ."

"No, you're right, it's a good idea. I'm sure Ames'll be cool with it."

I tamp down the urge to throw a fit and tell her she's being selfish . . . because the truth is she's not. I didn't *tell* her I'd rather be home than at Reenzie's, so it's stupid to think she'd want to stay home by herself when Erick and I are both going out. And the photo album shows it pretty clearly—Halloween was her and Dad's holiday long before it belonged to all of us. If I were her, I'd probably want to run away from it too.

I'm just upset because I had a wish, and I'd hoped it would come true.

As soon as I can, I run back upstairs and get dressed. I grab the journal and toss it into a purse, then call J.J.

"Hey," I say. "Any chance you're up for giving me a ride to my grandmother's?"

"As you wish," he says.

He gets to the house so fast I'm still putting on my makeup when he rings the bell. By the time I get downstairs, Mom's foisted a muffin on him and they're bent over the newspaper together so he can help her with the crossword.

"I'm taking back my friend, Mom," I say. "You can have Erick's."

"He won't stay your friend if you make him drive you everywhere," Mom says. "Amanda told me about a fantastic driving instructor she used for her son. I want you to give her a try."

I roll my eyes. "I'll think about it."

"I don't mind driving her, Mrs. Falls," J.J. says.

"See?" I say. "He doesn't mind."

We're in the car before J.J. asks, "You didn't tell her?"

"She should know," I say.

J.J. nods and lets it go. He turns up the music. Then he turns it down again. "She probably doesn't want to think about it. But if you *told* her, she'd get it. Then she'd stop bugging you."

"Or she'd stick me in therapy," I say, "which would be a waste, because it's not like there's some deep dark mystery. My dad died in a car crash. I don't want to drive. Done."

"Right," J.J. agrees. "Except, you know, a therapist would have you work through it and—"

"Change things so my dad *didn't* die in a car crash?" I ask.

J.J. turns red. I feel like a jerk because I'm being difficult on purpose, but really, I don't want to talk about it.

"No," J.J. says tightly. "You're right."

"I think you're just sick of being my chauffeur," I tease him.

"Madam, it is my unbridled honor and privilege to be your chauffeur," he says. "Should we be so lucky as to go to college in the same vicinity, I will happily continue to be your chauffeur even then."

"Totally want that in writing," I say. "And after college?"

"Goes without saying."

We pull up to Century Acres, the residence my grandmother moved to after she had her stroke last year. I pop out, wave goodbye to J.J., and run in. It's a big sprawling building, but Eddy's always in the lobby listening to the day's entertainment, in the dining room eating, in the activity room playing bingo, or in her room. Today it's the lobby, but Eddy isn't happy. Her small brown body with the cotton tuft of white hair is swallowed by the chair she's in, and she clings to the arms with a clawlike grip.

She's glaring up at a similarly tiny woman, who could be Eddy's negative image. This woman is just as old and just as tiny, but her wispy corona of hair is black, and her skin is chalky white as opposed to Eddy's nut-brown. They're even dressed the opposite of one another: Eddy's in a black T-shirt over white sweatpants; the other woman wears a white button-down blouse over black high-water slacks.

The other woman also wears glasses . . . but as jewelry. They hang around her neck on a chain. Seems to me to defeat the purpose of glasses, but then again I'm not old, so what do I know.

Actually, as I move closer, I realize I *do* know one thing—this woman is screaming at my grandmother.

"This is *my* seat!" she screeches. "I *always* sit here before dinner!"

Let the record show that it's now two o'clock in the afternoon. I just had breakfast. They're prepping for the dinner they're going to eat in about two hours.

"You think I don't know that?" my grandmother shoots back. "This is the most comfortable chair in the whole building and you hog it every day. Not this time. I got here right after lunch, and I'm not moving. And don't think you're getting me up for a bathroom break, because I'm wearing supplies."

I squeeze my eyes shut as I try to erase that last part from my mind, then move closer to the fracas. I notice there's a guy around my age holding the other woman's arm. I wonder if he's a relative or volunteer trying to break up the fight. "Hi, Eddy," I say, then ask a question I'm not sure I want answered. "What's going on?"

"Autumn! *Carina!* Come down here so I can kiss you."

I bend down and let her give me a too-wet kiss on the cheek.

"I'd get up," she says, "but then this vulture would swoop into my seat."

"*My* seat!" the vulture squawks. "You stole it!"

"It doesn't belong to you!" Eddy shoots back.

"Excuse me," the guy holding the vulture's arm says. He has a baseball cap pulled low over his face, but I can still see he's giving Eddy a sweet and charming smile. "Mrs. Falciano?"

"*Sí.* But if you think you score points knowing my name, you're wrong," Eddy says.

I don't know, I'm pretty impressed he knows Eddy's name. I don't know the names of anyone else around here.

The guy's smile doesn't falter. If anything, his voice gets kinder. "You did say that you know my grandmother always sits there . . . and that you sat down specifically to take the seat from her, right?"

"*Sí* . . . ," Eddy says suspiciously.

"So it's reasonable to say that you *did* steal the seat from her, right?" he asks. "And we all know stealing's wrong, so—"

"Whoa whoa whoa!" I jump in. "Does your grandmother own this place?"

The guy looks up at me like he only just realized I'm here. There's something familiar about his face, but I don't want to figure out what it is—I'm too angry that he's trying to manipulate Eddy into giving up her seat.

Now he's trying to do the same to me. He gives me the same overly kind smile and uses the same tone, like I'm a little kid throwing a tantrum. "No, of course she doesn't own it."

"Stop it," I say. "Don't talk to me that way. Be real. It's not your grandmother's place, so it's not her chair."

The guy drops the condescending tone. Now when he talks, he sounds annoyed. "I know it's not her chair, but is it such a big deal to let her sit there? Your grandmother's been there for hours."

"Because *your* grandmother's *always* there!" I shoot back.

A voice in the back of my head starts screaming at me to shut up because it just realized something, but I don't pay attention. I'm too furious. "Do you have any idea how many times my grandmother's complained to me because she never gets a chance to sit in the only comfortable chair in this place?"

"Do you have any idea how many times *my* grandmother's complained to me about the woman who stands over her glaring at her all afternoon when she's just trying to sit down and rest?"

The two old women are watching us like we're a tennis match, but I'm not even paying attention to them anymore. I'm all about this guy and putting him in his place.

"Your grandmother's a seat hog," I say.

"Yours is a bully!"

"*You're* the bully! If I hadn't come in here, you'd have conned my grandmother out of her seat when she has just as much of a right to be there as yours!"

The guy's grandmother gasps and moves in front of her grandson like she's going to shield him, which is pretty ridiculous since her head barely comes up to his chest. "You can't talk to my grandson that way!" she snaps. "He's a *superstar.*"

Eddy scoffs out loud. "You think *my* granddaughter isn't a superstar? They're all superstars to us!"

But my jaw's on the floor because I just realized what that voice in the back of my head was trying to tell me. There's a very good reason the guy looks familiar to me. It would be shocking if his face *didn't* look familiar to me, since I've been gazing at it longingly for almost three years.

I open my mouth to speak, but nothing comes out.

I'm fighting over a Century Acres chair ... with *Kyler Leeds.*

4

"No," Kyler Leeds's grandmother snaps at Eddy, "*my* grandson is an *actual* superstar. He's on the radio. He's on TV. He's in the paper. He does movies."

Kyler puts his hands gently on his grandmother's shoulders and smiles like he's embarrassed. "I haven't done movies, Meemaw."

He glares up at me at that last part, like he's afraid I'm about to pull out my phone and post to Twitter @Kyler Leeds calls his grandmother Meemaw! #soooadorable

Which I totally am, by the way. After I figure out how to turn this around so he doesn't completely hate my guts, which would be a problem since he's destined to fall hopelessly in love with me.

"I don't care if your grandson *has* done movies," Eddy retorts, "and neither does my granddaughter. Right, Autumn?"

"Well . . ." I stall as I try to find an expression for my face that's something resembling normal.

"I bet neither one of us has ever even heard of him," Eddy continues. "I don't know a single superstar with the last name Rubenstein."

"That's because he has a different last name," his grandmother snaps. "He's *Kyler Leeds*." Then she turns to me. "And I bet you *have* heard of him, right?"

Eddy laughs out loud before I can answer. She's so giddy she releases her claw grip and relaxes back in the chair cushions. "Kyler Leeds? Oh, she's heard of him. She won a prize on a TV show to spend an evening with him and you know what she did? She dumped him off on her friends because she didn't want to be around such a talentless *panzon*!"

Oh crap. I forgot I'd told Eddy that story. I know I didn't tell it to her *that* way, but still . . .

Eddy's still cackling in the chair. I feel my face grow hot. I close my eyes and cringe. When I open them, Kyler has a strange look on his face.

"That was you?" he asks.

"Um . . . yeah," I admit. I shift uncomfortably from one foot to the other and wonder if I can steal one of the geriatrics' scooters and bug out of here.

Then Kyler smiles. "It's really great to meet you."

"It is?"

"Yeah," he laughs. "Your friends told me a lot about you. I was really impressed by what you did for them. It was cool."

New planned tweet: @KylerLeeds thinks I'm cool!!!! #totallydying

"Thanks," I say.

His smile fades. "Of course, that was before I found out you think I'm a talentless *panzon*."

Face getting hot again. "I swear I didn't say that!" I lower my voice so my grandmother won't be embarrassed, and add, "Eddy got it a little mixed up. She does that sometimes. . . ."

Kyler laughs out loud. "It's okay. I get it." He says that with a glance down at his grandmother, and I smile because I realize he *does* get it. For a second he's not Kyler Leeds; he's just a really cute guy who's dealing with something really similar to me.

Then my insides start freaking out again. Even to my own ears, my voice actually sounds shaky when I try to sound casual and ask, "So what are you doing *here*?"

"He's visiting his Meemaw, what do you think?" his grandmother says, reaching up and taking his hand. "Because he's a good boy."

"Thanks, Meemaw." He leans down and kisses the top of her head. "I rent a place down here whenever I can, between tours and stuff. I like to be around for her."

"Oh yeah," I say. "Me too. For Eddy, I mean."

Eddy snorts a little too loudly. "So what are we doing about the chair?" she says. "You two are all chummy now, but a minute ago this one was trying to take my seat!"

"Tell you what," Kyler says. "Meemaw, let me take you out. We'll see a movie, and we'll get dinner someplace with way more comfortable seats than this one. Deal?"

"Deal."

"Great. Give me one sec. You start, I'll catch up with you."

His grandmother nods and starts shuffling toward the door. At her pace, she could give him an hour and he'd still catch up with her. "Autumn," he says.

Kyler Leeds just said my name. In person, right in front of me. Talking to me.

Which probably means I should answer.

"Yeah?"

He beckons me close, and I wonder if he's going to invite me to join them for dinner . . . or join him for a quick trip to Paris. Something little like that.

He looks around as if making sure no one's listening, which is pretty funny since his grandmother was screaming his name a second ago. He speaks in a low whisper, and I can feel his breath against my cheek.

"Can you do me a huge favor and not tell anybody about this? Everyone here has been really good about it, and I don't want it to turn into some kind of paparazzi thing when I come and visit my grandmother, you know?"

"Totally, I get it. I won't say a word."

I wonder if tweeting counts as saying. Probably does.

"Thanks. I'll see you around." He grins. "And I'll try to get Meemaw to be cooler about the chair thing."

I return the smile. "I'll talk to Eddy too."

He trots the five feet to catch up to his grandmother. When I turn to Eddy, she's already half out of her chair.

"Good, she's gone," she huffs. "I lied about the supplies. I need to pee like a racehorse."

♥

A half hour and a string of frenzied, sworn-to-secrecy texts with Jenna later, Eddy and I are perched in chairs in her room. I lean forward and anxiously watch her run her fingers over its blank cover.

"Why did he go?" I ask softly, the words thick in my mouth.

Eddy shrugs. "The way of the Taino . . . it's a mystery."

I look down at my fingers and pick at the edges of my gel polish—turquoise in honor of yesterday's football game. "I did some things with the diary that weren't so great," I admit. "Do you think . . . do you think he left because he's mad at me?"

"Oh, *querida*." Eddy sighs with a sad smile. She lays down the journal and takes my hands. "Your father, he loves you very much. A little mistake . . . a *big* mistake . . . that wouldn't send him away. If you need him, he's there."

"But he's not. You see it yourself. The symbol's gone. And when I wrote in it, nothing happened." My voice drops to just above a whisper when I say the last part. "He left me."

"He left you with a *mission*," Eddy clarifies. "*¿Sí?*"

"Peace and harmony, little corner of the world. Yeah," I say mechanically.

"Then if you need his help, he's there. Maybe you just need to look a little harder."

I'd need a microscope to look harder. The symbol is gone. That's obvious. And it's just as obvious that Eddy isn't going to help get it back. I hang out with her while she finds an acceptable hoodie for dinner in the dining room—this one is for a CrossFit studio and I have no idea how it ended up in my grandmother's closet—then call J.J. "Not trying to abuse the chauffeur privilege," I say, "but if you're around and available . . ."

"As you wish," he says. "Be there in five."

He's there in four. By five I'm already in seat-tilted-back, shoes-off, feet-on-dash position.

"Seems to me it's a complete waste of a new car and a driver's license if we don't go someplace different every day," J.J. says. "If you look in the dashboard, you'll see I made a list."

That involves shifting from my feet-up position, but I do it anyway. "Monkey Jungle?" I ask. "Is that a thing?"

J.J. nodded. "So's Butterfly World. I also include things like the mall, the beach, and the movies, not just the ones close by but within a four-hour radius."

I flip over the single page of notebook paper. "This is a very short list for all that."

"It's a list in progress."

"Disney World?" I see it on the last line on the back of the page. "Let's go there now!"

"Family dinner tonight, otherwise I would. Pick another."

I'm still looking at the sheet when Amalita calls me and Jack calls J.J., so we pick them up before we go. Taylor's at *Guys and Dolls* rehearsal, and Reenzie and Sean are doing homework—which the rest of us should probably be doing too, but this is way more fun. It's torture not to spill to Amalita about Kyler Leeds, but she's not like Jenna. She's as huge a fan as I am, and even if she swore to me she'd be cool, she'd totally stalk Century Acres to see him again. I can even imagine her dressing up as a little old lady and having J.J. push her in a rented wheelchair so she could try to fit in. It's something I have to admit I'd love to see, but Kyler would kill me, so I keep it quiet.

We let Ames choose the destination from J.J.'s list. She picks Butterfly World, so we drive a half an hour to this really beautiful place filled with massive outdoor gardens that are netted so the butterflies don't escape. They fly free in there and can even land on you, which totally freaks Jack out. I Instagram like twenty pictures of him twisting and contorting as he dances around trying to get butterflies off his arms, chest, and back without actually swatting them. Then we move into the Lorikeet Encounter, where you can buy tiny cups of nectar and the lorikeets—these parakeet-sized birds with bright green bodies and blue heads—swoop down to eat it. I get a picture of Ames with three on her head, and J.J. snaps one of me with a lorikeet on each of my shoulders. Jack is too traumatized from the butterflies and refuses to come in, but J.J. convinces him it'll be fine, that he doesn't have to bring in nectar and the birds won't even notice him, and besides, we need him to take a picture of the rest of us with lorikeets on our heads. It takes forever, but he finally agrees to come in . . . and we pour cups of nectar on him so the birds dive-bomb him like vultures on a lion's leftovers.

Not that they bite him or anything. They're very tame. That's why it's so funny. Jack's screaming and wailing because he's tackled by basically a bunch of winged kittens.

We get kicked out after that, but it's totally worth it. And I get a ton of pictures, the best of which I immediately Snapchat to Sean, Taylor, and Reenzie.

Jack's revenge is he won't sit on the towel J.J. gives him. He cuddles his bird-poo-stained body right into the upholstery. J.J. swears it's worth the car wash bill.

When I get home, I really need to work. We started reading *Les Misérables* in English, and so far I've succeeded in opening the front cover, then downloading and watching the Hugh Jackman musical, which we all loved (except for Russell Crowe, who sings like I read), but Reenzie tells me that doesn't count as reading the book. First, though, I have to tell Mom all about Butterfly World, because I'd texted her the picture of me with the birds on my shoulders. She's entranced and wants to have a family outing there immediately, but I'm pretty sure I've already had the peak Butterfly World experience. Plus, my friends and I are banned for life. Still, the whole thing was so fun I nearly forget about the missing *zemi*, until I see Erick and almost blurt out, *I'm sorry I accused you of stealing my journal.*

That would have been seriously weird, since I only accused him in my head. Plus, it would have clued him in that I *have* a journal, at which point he totally *would* steal it.

Still, it gets me thinking about the journal and how Eddy said I should look a little harder, so I excuse myself after dessert and go up to my room. I check my phone first. Sean and Reenzie both texted about the Jack/lorikeet picture.

> **REENZIE:** I am totally having lorikeets at my Halloween party next week.

> **SEAN:** Can't talk. Stuffing lorikeets in Jack's locker.

Both funny . . . and both kind of similar, which gives me evil suspicious thoughts of them sitting together and gazing into one another's eyes as they composed the texts, then only reluctantly letting go of each other's hands so they could type and send them . . . but that's pure paranoia.

I flop onto my bed and pull the journal out of my bag. The cover is exactly the way it was this morning: blank. How am I supposed to look closer? I hold the thing right up to my face; I shine the flashlight from my phone on it . . . nothing. Then I Google "hidden places in books," which takes me to a site about secret compartments you can make out of books, coins, watches, and clocks, all of which I clearly need immediately. Google is a bottomless hole of awesome distraction on this one, so I put my phone down and go back to the journal. I flip the pages next to my ear, like I'm a safecracker in a movie and it'll tell me its secrets, but I only succeed in blowing an irritating gust of wind into my eardrum.

Now I'm ready to give up. I flop onto my side and absently peel back the front cover of the book. Slowly, like I'm raising a backbone one vertebra at a time. The cover's pliable—I've rolled it back like this before; it's something I do with my hands sometimes when I have it out and I'm on the phone. Like doodling.

Only this time I notice the cover doesn't roll. It goes back in a single, unbending flap, perfectly flat.

I sit up straight and flap the cover, back and forth.

No bend.

That's weird.

I specifically try to peel it back slowly and roll it, but it doesn't happen. The front cover is stiff. When I rub the cover between my fingers, it feels like something's *inside* it—something hard and rectangular between the leather and whatever worn, pliable material it's wrapped around.

That's new.

I look closely at the cover, but there's no sign of a cut. It doesn't look like anyone sliced into it to place something inside . . . but something's there.

This, of course, is impossible.

Just like it's impossible for a journal to grant wishes. And impossible for an embossed *zemi* to fade off a book.

I need to get inside the cover. I run downstairs. Mom and Erick are both in their rooms, so no one but Schmidt sees me as I rummage through Mom's junk drawer and take out an X-Acto knife. As I race it back to my room, I can't help but imagine myself tripping and stabbing myself with it, but thankfully that doesn't happen. I also don't slice off my thumb as I run the blade gently around the front cover. The knife is sharp and slices through the leather so easily that I soon peel back a huge flap that hangs like dead skin.

Ugh—that's a nasty image. I must be hanging out with Jack too much.

I don't linger on it. Something else has my attention. Sticking out behind the flap—tucked between the leather and the piece of soft, worn cardboard that gives the cover its shape—is a piece of plastic, matchbook-thick. I tweeze its edge with my thumb and forefinger and pull it out. It's just a little smaller than the book cover itself—big enough that my flat hand would fit inside with a couple inches all around. It's blue, with a blob of green printed in the middle. When I turn it over I gasp.

The three-point *zemi* is printed there.

I call Jenna immediately.

"If you're calling to tell me you're running away with

Kyler Leeds," she says, "I'm registering an official complaint."

"I found another *zemi*," I say, "and you wouldn't complain because Kyler Leeds is my destiny."

I tell her about the sheet of material and text a picture of it.

"It looks sort of like a map," Jenna says. "Like Australia surrounded by the ocean."

"My dad wants me to go to Australia? I'm totally on that! I would love to hold a koala bear!"

"Highly doubt your dad's sending you to Australia," Jenna says. "Besides, it doesn't look quite like that."

"Oh! Maybe it's an exotic island," I say. "Maybe Dad wants me to go to Maui. Or Jamaica. Or Bermuda."

"Maybe you could scan it into the computer and see what place it matches," Jenna suggests, which sounds great in theory but is actually way too complicated for me. I can scan, but I'd have no idea how to get the computer to read the scan and tell me if it looks like anyplace specific. Luckily, I know someone who loves that kind of thing.

"Erick!" I say after I hang up with Jenna, cruise into his room, and plop down on his bed. "What's up?"

He's on his computer—handy for me—and is editing some video he shot of himself and Aaron.

"Aaron thinks you're hot," he says without looking up from his screen.

"Ew!"

"Yeah. I told him he's an idiot."

"Thank you," I say. "I think."

"He still thought you were hot, so I showed him that video of you from when Amalita and Taylor slept over and you were all playing Heads Up."

"What? You *videotaped* us?"

"You weren't in your room. The family room's a public area. Plus, I did you a favor. After he saw it, Aaron agreed you're pretty dorky. Now he likes Amalita."

I take a deep breath. "Okay. I'm going to kill you, but first I'm going to get your help."

"Why would I help you if you're going to kill me afterward?"

"If you don't help me, I'll kill you."

"No deal. Doesn't end well for me either way."

I clench my teeth. "*If* you help me, I *won't* kill you."

"I'm in," he says, and spins around to face me. "What's up?"

I hand him the plastic piece as casually as possible, as if it weren't at all meaningful to me. "I found this thing that looks kind of like a map, and I want to know what it's a map of."

"Mr. Weirdo Happy Face?" He's looking at the *zemi*.

"Turn it over," I say.

"Huh," he says, and I can tell I've piqued his interest. He scans it into his computer, and while he taps stuff out on his keyboard, I look around the room. I really should be nicer to Erick; he'll probably be supporting me one day. He has cameras everywhere—old-school film ones as well as the regular kind—and props he's made for the mini-movies he's always shooting and editing. The posters on the walls are ones he created for his own films, tricked out to look like real posters you'd see in a theater. One wall is completely covered with dry-erase boards so he can keep track of all his projects.

Of course, since I'll be with Kyler Leeds, I don't have to worry about Erick supporting me. I can make him miserable; I bet he'll still thank me in his Oscar speech.

"I've got it," he says. He takes the plastic off his scanner bed and holds it up. "It's nothing."

"What do you mean?"

"It doesn't match anything real. Plus, it feels like dry-erase material." He taps it. "So I guess it's like a game or something. You write stuff on it and then erase it and write stuff on it again. Pretty lame game, though."

He wheels his desk chair across the room and grabs one of his dry-erase pens from a board shelf.

"What are you doing?" I ask him.

"Writing on it," he says. "I'll call it ERICKDONIA and put it up on my door."

I whip the pen and the plastic out of his hand. "No, you won't. It's mine!"

"It's nothing, though!" Erick says. "What are you going to do with it?"

"Something," I say, which seems like a pretty definitive final word on the subject, so I storm back to my own room and shut and lock the door. I call Jenna back and tell her what Erick said.

"Is he right?" Jenna asks. "Is it dry-erase?"

I still have Erick's dry-erase pen, so I make a little mark on the map and then wipe it away with my finger.

"Yeah . . . but I still have no idea what it is. Or why my dad would want me to have it."

Jenna can't figure it out either, and soon we're talking about other things. She's a stress case these days because she's like Reenzie and totally focused on college. Jenna wants to get a running scholarship to the University of Oregon, which apparently churns out superstar runners on a daily basis, but she's also taking three AP courses, already freaking about the three she plans to take next year, and she is dealing with Grand High Drama over a guy she just broke up with who refuses to get the hint and go away.

I still have the dry-erase pen in my hand, and doodle while she fills me in. I make little circles, then wipe them away . . . little smiley faces . . . my own version of the three-point *zemi*—which looks weirdly like Homer Simpson. Then I scrawl Jenna's name across the green fake landmass on the map . . .

. . . and scream, because I'm suddenly sprawled on Jenna's bed, watching her pace around the room talking to me.

5

Jenna wheels around at the sound of my voice, and she screams too. Both in front of me and in my ear—we're still holding our cell phones. I hang mine up. She drops hers on the floor.

"Jenna?" her dad's voice booms from his room down the hall. "Are you okay?"

Jenna's eyes are saucers and beneath her bedtime shorts and tank top her tan skin has gone pale as mine. She doesn't take her eyes off me, but she has the where-withal to shout, "It's okay, Dad—I just saw a bug!"

"You need me to get it?" Jenna's mom's voice rings down. I love that in Jenna's house it's her mom who's the resident bug-killer.

"No, I'm good!" Jenna yells. "I got it!"

She races to the bed and crouches down in front of me. "How are you here?"

"I have no idea," I say. "I wrote your name on the map. . . ."

A chill floods over me. The map!

"Right there," Jenna says.

The map's right in front of me on the bed. I wasn't holding it, but it came with me. I have no clue how, but that seems like the least of the moment's impossibilities. Jenna picks it up and sits next to me on the bed so we can both look at it.

"Where?" she says.

I'd written it right across the green landmass, but it's not there anymore. "It erased," I say.

"Or soaked in," Jenna says, "when it brought you here."

There is no one else in the universe like Jenna. She's crazy smart and so rational it hurts, but when her best friend magically and impossibly appears on her bed, she doesn't even bother looking for a logical reason. She jumps right to the *illogical* but only reasonable solution: the map brought me.

"So that's what the map does," I marvel. "It brings me to people." I think about it a second, then gasp. "I could go see Kyler Leeds *right now*!"

"You *don't* want to pop into Kyler Leeds's room out of nowhere," Jenna says, "especially when he knows who you are. He'll think you're a crazed stalker."

I bob my head from side to side, weighing the label in my mind.

"Yes, I know you *are* his crazed stalker," Jenna says, "but you don't want him to know that or he'll call the cops."

"Still might be worth it," I say.

Jenna rolls her eyes. "Then you'll never see him again and you'll lose your destiny."

That clinches it. "Not Kyler, then. Who should I go see?"

A whole list of people runs through my head, from celebrities to my school principal, Ms. Dorio, who's the most uptight woman I've ever met. I'd love to peek in and see what she does on a Saturday night.

"Stop, stop," Jenna says. "You need to be careful about this. This is amazing, but it's like the journal. It's powerful, and it can get you into huge trouble."

I nod. When I first started using the journal, Jenna told me about "The Monkey's Paw," a short story about wishes that came true but with horrible consequences. If I'd listened to her then, I probably would have saved myself a lot of agony. "Okay," I say. "What do we do? How do I use it?"

Jenna hops back up so she can pace. Her ponytail swishes against her back with every step. Jenna always thinks better in motion.

"Well, you wrote down my name and you got to me. . . ." She freezes and gasps. "How will you get home? You're a thousand miles away from Florida. How are you going to explain to your mom that you're here?"

"The map will get me back, right?"

"How? Write down your mom's name? What if you show up in bed with her when she's sitting up watching TV?"

I laugh out loud, picturing her face if I just appeared in bed next to her.

"I'm serious!" Jenna says. "Or what if you write down Erick's name and—"

"Stop," I cut her off. "Erick's a twelve-year-old walking hormone. I don't want to be anywhere near what he does alone in his room at night."

"Ew," Jenna agrees.

"I could write down Schmidt's name."

"He could be in the room with Erick or your mom."

"I could write down my own name," I suggest. "Maybe that would take me to my room?"

"Try it."

I still have the dry-erase marker in my hand. I'm shaking a little, but I scrawl *Autumn* across the green patch. I close my eyes and wait to disappear.

"You're still here," Jenna finally says.

"I am?" I snap my eyes open. She's right.

"I just realized something," she says. "There's a lot of Jennas and a lot of Autumns. How did you get to *me*, and how did you not just end up next to some other girl named Autumn?"

She has a point. I chew on a strand of my hair and think it over.

"Well . . . if the *zemi* holds some part of my dad's spirit," I say, "it's not dumb. It probably knows which person I mean, even if I don't spell it out."

"That makes sense."

She says it so seriously that I snort laughing, because

sense is the last thing any of this makes. She laughs too, but still picks up one of her pillows and hurls it at me. "Shut up! You know what I mean. Okay, so if the map has an idea of what's on your mind, how do you think it would get you home?"

Her eyes meet mine, and I know what she's saying. I nod to her cell phone, which is still on the floor where she dropped it. "Grab your phone," I say as I tuck my own in my pocket. "I'll call you."

I uncap the pen and write *Home* on the map . . .

. . . and suddenly I'm coughing because I'm under my bed and I haven't dusted in, oh, ever.

I roll out and dial Jenna's number, but I'm still coughing.

"Are you okay?" she screeches when she hears me. "Is there a fire?"

"Is there a *fire*? Wouldn't I be screaming if there was a fire?"

"I thought the coughing . . . Forget it. Where are you?"

"My room. Coughing from the dust bunnies under the bed. Dust bunnies, by the way, nowhere near as cute as actual bunnies."

"This is amazing," Jenna says, and I can tell from her voice she's smiling super-wide.

Then I remember I don't have to tell from her voice.

"Can I come back over?" I ask.

"YES!" she whisper-shouts. "Oh my gosh, you can come over all the time! It'll be like you never moved! Yes!"

I write her name on the map and pop right back to her room. We spend the rest of the night testing out exactly how the map works. It seems pretty clear that if I write down someone's name, I show up right around wherever that person is. Home gets me back to my room. For other places, I just name them, like Jenna's kitchen pantry or Jenna's basement or Jenna's tire swing.

I do run into a couple of problems. At one point I start writing before I really know what I want to say. I know I want to try somewhere that *isn't* on Jenna's property, but close by. Somewhere else in the development. I start by writing the word "Outside," but I'm still thinking about the next word and I guess I take too long because I end up *I have no idea where,* up to my knees in snow, in the middle of a blizzard. I quickly write myself back to Jenna's room and promise myself to be extra careful . . . although I don't account for my dyslexia. Close to dawn I try writing Dog park and only figure out I wrote God park when I end up on a path with nothing around me except this big rock. When I shine my phone flashlight on it, I see the words "Garden of the Gods." When I write my way back to Jenna, she looks it up on Google. It's a state park in Colorado.

Yikes.

The map's dangers are pretty clear.

What's not clear is why Dad gave it to me.

"Maybe he knew you needed more time back in Maryland?" Jenna suggests.

Maybe . . . but if that was the case, I'd have gotten the

map *before* the diary. Back then was when I really needed Stillwater time. Now, even though I miss Jenna, Aventura's home.

We don't figure it out before dawn, and by that time we're both zombies. I give Jenna a huge hug before I write myself home, and fall asleep immediately. I dream I'm a superhero, flying around the world and soaring into a situation just in time to save the day. I break into locked cars and pull out babies and dogs before they boil to death; I show up at the scene of tiny brushfires and put them out before they burn acres of land and houses; I appear at the top of Cinderella's Castle and watch the Disney World fireworks from the number one ultimate location. The last one isn't so much a superhero moment as it is really, really cool, but I wake up totally inspired. I text Jenna:

I have it! I am a superhero!

????? she texts back.

The map! I can go places and stop people from getting into trouble!

Jenna sends back a frowny-face emoji with the text Be careful . . .

I roll my eyes and tuck my phone away. I get that she's worried about me, but I know I'm right. It makes sense. Dad believed my mission is to bring peace and harmony to the world. What better way to bring peace and harmony to the world than by saving people's lives! I can be like a guardian angel! If Dad had someone like me show up the night of his crash and tell him not to drive, he'd still be alive today.

I want to get started right away, but then I realize it's already four in the afternoon. I slept all day. Mom's probably worried. I go downstairs and see that the house is empty, but there's a note on the kitchen table from Mom saying she hopes I feel okay, there's chicken soup in the fridge if I'm sick, and she and Erick will be home when they get out of the movies.

Perfect. I have time.

But how do I get to someone who needs me? The map doesn't tell the future—it's not like I can write on it, "Take me to someone who's about to get hurt so I can stop it from happening."

Can I?

I run back to my room and grab the map. I'm about to try it when I imagine myself appearing in a war zone, dodging bullets as I try to drag an injured soldier to safety.

Noble? Yes.

Terrifying and life-threatening? Also yes.

I remember the dog thing from my dream. That's simpler and clearer. I write on the map, *Inside a car with a dog locked in on a hot day.*

I show up in a sauna.

It's not a sauna, but it's a sweltering car. It's so hot I can barely breathe. I'm in the backseat, and next to me is a tiny

Pomeranian, a fuzzball of a dog. He's on his hind legs, his paws on the window, and there's condensation on the glass from all his panting.

My heart breaks and I immediately know I did the right thing.

"You poor little guy," I coo. "Let me help you."

I press the button to roll down the window a crack, but nothing happens.

Of course not. The car's off.

So I click the door handle, but it doesn't work either. Child lock?

I'm getting dizzy from the heat. I should have brought water with me.

"It's okay, puppy," I say soothingly. "I'll climb up front and open—"

That's when I hear the growls. By the time I turn around, the fuzzball has bared its fangs and it's an inch away from my face.

"Easy, puppy," I say with a smile. "I'm just trying to help. I'm like a superhero, get it?"

The dog doesn't get it. It lunges, and I only just manage to throw my arms over my face before the attack. The Pom might be tiny, but it's strong. I can feel its little teeth and claws gnawing through my clothes and scraping my arms, but I don't want to bat it away and hurt it, so I'm basically wrestling with a teeny tornado of fur and blades. Then I hear a deep male voice shouting outside the car.

"HEY!" it yells. "Who's in there? What's going on?"

I'd look and see who the guy is, but I don't want to get my eyes scratched out by the Pup of Doom. I somehow manage to twist my back to the dog and bend double while I write *Home* on the map. I hear the double-beep of the car unlocking and feel the cool rush of outside air just before I appear back on my bed.

"I am not a superhero," I say in a quavering voice. "I'm not."

I bring my phone as I stagger to the bathroom. I wasn't gone long—Mom and Erick are still at the movies—so I FaceTime Jenna while I clean out my scratches.

"Did the dog have its shots?" Jenna wonders.

"I didn't really get the chance to ask," I say. "It didn't break my skin, though. Not with its teeth." It scratched my arms like crazy, but nothing too deep. "Maybe this *zemi* isn't my dad's spirit at all," I say. "Maybe it's some evil spirit trying to mess with me."

Jenna shakes her head. "You forgot something. With the diary, Eddy said your dad wanted you to bring peace and happiness—"

"To the world," I finish. "I know. Which clearly I suck at doing."

"To *your little corner* of the world," Jenna reminds me. "Saving random people around the universe is great, Autumn, but it has nothing to do with your little corner of the world. It's too much."

"So how do I use the map to bring peace and harmony to my little corner of the world?" I ask.

"You already started," she says. "You came to visit me when I was totally stressed out and gave me the best night I've had since we left camp. And what about Ames and Taylor? Didn't you start with the diary because you wanted to help them?"

Jenna's right. That *is* why I'd pulled out the journal. Ames and Taylor are both pining for guys they can't get. Helping them is something I would have tried to do with the diary, so now I'll do it with the map. And I probably won't get clawed in the process.

Now I just have to figure out how.

6

It takes me a while to figure out how the map can help my friends' love lives. In the meantime I use it to make a couple of trips back to Jenna in Stillwater. She drives us to some stores a few towns over so we don't run into anyone who will recognize me, and she helps me pick out a costume for Reenzie's party on Saturday. I'm still nostalgic for the Halloweens I used to have, but Jenna promises me that if I get really depressed, I can call her. She's going to a party, but it's nothing big and she's happy to slip out if I need her.

Maybe keeping me close to Jenna this time of year *is* why Dad's spirit moved to the map. It's definitely helping me feel more peaceful about something I thought would be brutal.

The costume we pick out for me is nothing as ornate as the kinds of things my mom put together, but I like that. I want it to be simple and easy. I go with zombie bride. The dress is short and ripped, so I won't swelter in the Aventura humidity and I can dance in it. I get fake contacts that look bloodshot, and I buy a little paint-on fake blood and stick-on scars. My skin's already deathly pale, so that part's easy. When I tell my Aventura friends about the costume at lunch on the school lawn, they like it.

"Where'd you get it?" Taylor asks. "I didn't see that when I was looking."

"I got it online," I lie. Not a big lie. I could've gotten it online. I just happened to get it in Maryland.

"You know I love talking about my party," Reenzie says, getting up, "but I have to run. Yearbook meeting."

"Since when are you on the yearbook?" Sean laughs.

"Today's my first day," she says, "but it's part of my lifelong passion to be an archivist and record our fleeting young lives for all posterity. At least, that's what I'll say on my college applications."

"I thought you were telling colleges your lifelong passion was ending the tyranny of football teams with race-offensive names," I say.

"It was," Reenzie says, "but Ms. Dorio said this morning the name wasn't changing no matter what, and I can't have my passion be an epic fail."

"But your passion *can* be something you've never had any interest in until now?" Taylor asks.

"It's a newly discovered passion that made me realize my true calling as a teller of stories and chronicler of lives," she says grandly . . . and it's so ridiculous that the rest of us burst out laughing.

Reenzie isn't amused. She stands taller and purses her lips into a single line. "You should all be nice to me," she huffs. "Stay on my good side and I'll make sure you look good in all the candids. Piss me off and I can't be responsible for your eternal legacy. Jokes are immediate; yearbooks are forever."

"*Mira,* you can't be mad," Ames says through her last gasps of laughter. "Just listen to yourself! You sound *chiflada!*"

Reenzie doesn't like being called crazy. "*Chiflada* this," she snaps, which makes no sense. "Yale only accepts ten percent of legacies. *Legacies.* Even second- and third-tier schools are turning away straight-A students because they don't have a passion that makes them stand out. You think you can get away with being Little Miss and Mister Well-Rounded? You can't. And, no, Ames, that's not a fat thing."

"*¡Que te pasa!*" Ames cries. "When you tell *just me* it's not a fat thing, it becomes a fat thing!"

"You're not fat," Jack says.

"Still talking about it, still a fat thing," Ames says. "*Callate.*"

"I'm just saying, this is the year that counts," Reenzie points out. "By next fall, we're already filling out early-decision applications and the die is cast. Swallow that with your corn dogs."

She expertly tosses her hair and strides away.

"She's a real breath of fresh air," J.J. says.

"I like Reenzie now," Ames says, "I do . . . but she can still be a real *pendejo*."

"I don't have to worry about that stuff," Taylor says. "The best theater schools only care about your audition."

"We're all fine," Amalita says. "You'll go act, Sean will play football, J.J.'s grades will get him anywhere, Autumn will get in with her 'My Dad Died' essay—"

"Nice," J.J. says. "Very sensitive."

"It's true!" she says. "And as a PuertoMecuadorbano Jew, I'm a diversity board's dream come true."

"What about me?" Jack says.

"Oh, you're screwed. You'll stay here and work at Steak 'n Shake." Ames doesn't give Jack the chance to object. She turns to Sean. "Did you invite Denny to Reenzie's Halloween party?"

"Yeah," Sean says, "but he won't go. He doesn't do parties."

Ames flops dramatically back onto the grass, her bracelets and earrings jangling all the way. "*Ai*, this boy is killing me! Where is he?" She looks around the lawn. "I need to talk to him. I could convince him to go to the party, and by the end of it, he'll be eating out of my hand."

"Only if you're holding grass-fed beef or a salad," Sean says. "He only eats lean protein and vegetables."

"That's why he looks like him and you look like you," Ames says.

"Weren't you just the one complaining about body-image comments?" I ask.

"I'm round," she says. "It's different when I say it."

"I'm just saying," Sean says, "McNack goes off campus for lunch, he doesn't hang around school except for classes and football, and he's a senior, so you're not going to run into him in class. I'm all for you going after him, Ames. I just don't see how it's going to happen."

BLING!

Is that the sound of a lightbulb going on above my head?

Why, yes. Yes, it is.

I check my phone. There's still forty minutes left of lunch period.

"I have to go," I say.

I sling my backpack over my shoulder and bus my tray with lightning speed, then duck around the building and behind a row of bushes where I know I won't be seen. I have the map in my bag—I keep it and a dry-erase pen in a small cloth drawstring purse I dug out of my closet. Looking around one last time to make sure no one's watching, I pull out the map and pen and write across the green land-mass, Denny McNack.

Next thing I know, I'm toppling off a high stool at a juice bar. There are only three customers: two in line, and one at a counter that faces outside. The workers are busy looking down at their blenders or the cash registers . . . or at least, I guess they were before I appeared, because no one screams and accuses me of being some kind of ghost or witch for popping into existence out of nowhere. But they are looking at me now, since I'm on the floor in a tangle of chair legs.

"I'm okay," I tell everyone. "Just slipped. All good."

No one cares. They go back to what they were doing. Including the guy at the counter, who is *totally* Denny McNack!

"Hey!" I say as if we're old friends.

He doesn't even turn around. Why would he? He's a senior football hero with one foot already in a college stadium. I'm not even on his radar. Maybe if I say I'm his quarterback's girlfriend . . .

. . . which would be a lie *and* might get back to Sean, who would wonder how I got here when I was just at lunch.

Wherever here is.

"Denny!" I try again. This time he turns. And while my heart is completely owned by Sean, and to a more long-term extent by Kyler Leeds, my knees go a little weak. I completely get why Amalita is obsessed with this guy, and I am in awe that she thinks she can snag him just by hanging out with him for a few minutes. Dark hair, dark eyes, chiseled face, every muscle in sight cut and sleek and . . .

I have a job to do. It's my second attempt at being a superhero—granted, a different kind of superhero—and this time I'm not going to mess it up.

"Great game last Friday," I say. "I'm a big fan."

He gives me a half-smile and a nod.

"Thanks."

Wow, even his voice is hot. Ames will love me forever when this works out. Of course, I can't tell her how I was secretly behind it, but that's how we superheroes roll.

"Yeah!" I enthuse. "It's so funny seeing you here . . . at this place . . ." I scan the room for logos, see one on the wall. "Loosey Juicey!"

This place is far too healthy for me to have heard of it. It smells like a meadow. I have no earthly clue where we are.

"Is this the one on . . . Melville? Down the street from the school?"

Denny looks less sexy when he stares at you like you're insane. "You're here," he says. "You're telling me you don't know where you are?"

"The fall," I say. "Tumbled off that stool. Little mixed up. Can you just tell me . . . ?"

He scrunches his face like he smells something bad. This from a guy who eats in a meadow. "Fourth and Avalon."

"Right! Of course! And, uh . . ." I lean over to check out his plate. It's piled in ground cover, and his glass is full of something green enough to be nuclear waste. "You're still eating, clearly, so I'll leave you to it . . . 'cause you'll probably be here for at least another . . . what . . . half hour?"

"Something like that," he says. "You take care now."

With that he turns his back on me, which is great because I don't need him to think I'm cool; I just need his location. Oh, sure, it'll be awkward when he's in love with

Ames and hanging out with all of us, but by then I'll have come up with an ingenious cover story that everyone will find endlessly charming.

I run outside and duck behind a mailbox, then pull out the map and write *Amalita* on it.

I pop into place at the edge of the lunch field. Again, no one sees me actually burst into existence, and since that's way too coincidental, I'm thinking it's part of the map's magic. It'll put me someplace awkward and possibly inexplicable, but it won't look to anyone that I've been playing with a *Star Trek* transporter, a reference I swear I only know because of Jack.

Ames and the gang—except go-getter Reenzie—are all right where I left them. I don't have a lot of time. I run over. "Ames! Tee! I just saw on Twitter that Kyler Leeds was seen in Aventura!"

"What! Where?"

"Are you kidding me?!"

"Around Fourth and Avalon, but we have to go *now*!"

"Do we have time?" Amalita checks her watch.

"Just enough," I say, "but we have to hurry."

"I'll drive," Ames says.

I shake my head. "Taylor. Your car's faster."

I have no idea if Taylor's car is faster, but I'm hoping Amalita has a different ride back to school than we do. Ames and Taylor go along with it, and we run to the parking lot and pile into the car. I sit in the backseat and fervently hope we don't *actually* find Kyler Leeds, since I promised I wouldn't say he's in town.

It takes five minutes to get to Fourth and Avalon, which is way longer than when I just burst over there.

"Slow down, slow down!" I say when we get close to the juice place. "Look in the windows—maybe he's in one of the stores."

I'm prepared to make the "discovery" if Ames doesn't notice Denny in the window, but it turns out I don't have to.

"*¡Dios mio!*" she gasps. "Stop the car!"

Taylor does and Ames leaps out. She leans back only long enough to say, "You can keep looking—I'll text if I need a ride."

As Taylor slowly drives on, I watch Ames shake out her hair, shimmy her dress into place, and sashay into Loosey Juicey. Mission accomplished.

"Did the tweet say anything else about him?" Taylor asks anxiously.

"Who?"

"*Kyler Leeds!* Did it say where exactly they saw him?"

"Oh yeah." I pretend to check my phone. "Shoot. Another tweet just said he already left the area."

"That sucks! I totally wanted to tell him about *Guys and Dolls.*" Then she laughs. "Like he'd actually remember me. I'm sure he has a million random nights with fans."

"Oh, he totally remembers you and Ames," I say . . . then immediately wish I hadn't.

"Yeah, right," Taylor scoffs. She doesn't consider for a second that I know something; she just thinks I'm being nice. Better that way.

Taylor cruises around for fifteen minutes looking for Kyler just in case the tweet was wrong and he's still in the area . . . which as far as I know he never was. We're about to call Ames and tell her if she wants a ride back to school we need to do it now, when both our phones chirp. It's a text from Ames. A selfie of her and Denny. Smiling. Inside his car. No doubt on their way back to school.

Taylor's amazed. I just lean back and smile.

It's good to be a superhero.

7

"She is unbelievable," I marvel to Taylor before U.S. History. It's the last class period of the day, and we're in the same section. Amalita has already texted us both that in the brief time she spent with Denny, she made such an impression that he asked her to go out with him after the game on Friday. It's an away game, so she's not cheering that night, but we'll all go and cheer on Sean . . . and Ames's insane powers of attraction.

"She's always been that way," Taylor says. "She's insanely picky, but when she turns it on, she gets who she wants. It's confidence. She's amazing."

"Maybe we could bottle it," I say.

"If we could, I'd use it on Ryan," she sighs. "It's brutal. We spend all this time together, and he acts like he really likes me, and he'll even put his arm around me and hold my hand . . . but it's not like we're together. He hasn't tried to kiss me. Not even close."

I raise an eyebrow.

"He's not gay," she says.

"Hey, I don't know him," I say. "If you tell me he's straight, he's straight."

"Straight and perfect," she says. "Wait till you see him in the show."

The teacher comes in and we stop talking, but then Taylor lights up and leans over. "Come to rehearsal after class! You can watch. Then you can see what I'm talking about."

Musical theater isn't so much my thing, and watching a rehearsal when I have nothing to do with the play will probably make me feel completely out of place. Plus, I have homework to do—I should just go home after school and get it done. But Taylor looks so excited about having me there that I say yes. I also realize it could be good for my superheroing. Maybe if I'm at rehearsal, I'll see a way to help Taylor and Ryan like I helped Amalita and Denny.

The cast of *Guys and Dolls* is still using their scripts and learning their choreography—the show isn't until December. But I watch a whole run-through complete with all the stops and starts as the director gives the cast ideas and tells them where to go onstage, and a couple things become totally clear.

I get it. Ryan Darby as Sky Masterson is incredibly sexy.

He's this bad-boy gambler who always has the right quip and who has this thick wall around him no girl can ever break through . . . until Sarah Brown, who's played by Taylor. It's impossible not to fall in love with Ryan as Sky. *I* fall in love with Ryan as Sky. Taylor's right. He's amazing. Genuinely meltworthy.

Then he steps out of character.

I don't like to stereotype. I don't. I don't believe in stereotyping. I don't like it. I don't do it. I'm not going to be like Reenzie, Jack, and J.J. and say Ryan is for-sure one-hundred-percent gay just because the second he stops being Sky he goes from intense and controlled to bouncy and theatrical. It doesn't mean he's gay when his speaking voice climbs three octaves. It is no litmus test of gayness that he can't seem to stand without draping an arm around another cast member, male or female. All I'm saying is that when you combine all that with the fact that he and Taylor have this super-intimate connection onstage and, according to Taylor, have one *off*stage and *still* aren't together in any kind of boyfriend/girlfriend way . . .

If it looks like a duck, swims like a duck, and quacks like a duck, in all likelihood it's a duck.

In this case, a gay duck.

Which is totally fine—I'm all for gay duckhood. It's just not ideal for my straight-duck friend who wants him.

So that's one thing that I learn at rehearsal. The other is that Taylor has a big-time secret admirer. He's sitting in the same row as me in the theater. He's cute: wire-rim glasses, short brown hair, jeans, and a plain black T-shirt. He watches everything intently, but whenever Taylor's on-stage, he leans a foot closer to the stage and he jiggles his knee up and down like he's really anxious. He also takes notes the whole time, so I know he's either doing something with the show or he's more spooky stalker than ad-mirer. I figure I should have my friend's back and learn which it is, so when the run-through ends and all the ac-tors are getting their notes, I move over three chairs and plop down next to him.

"Hey," I say. "Whatcha writing?"

"Me?" he asks, as if there's a whole row of people with pencils and notepads nearby instead of just him. He's gen-uinely asking, though, so I nod and smile.

"I do lighting," he says. "I'm taking notes on what gels will look best on which lights."

"Gels, like . . . what you put in your hair?"

He raises a hand to his head uncomfortably, like he thinks I'm insulting his hairdo.

"No," he says. "We put colored gels—thin pieces of plastic—over the stage lights. They set the mood, bring out the actors' features . . ."

He goes on, but I'm not listening to his words; I'm more listening to *him*. And watching him. There's something charmingly apologetic about him. He meets my eyes, but then he darts his gaze away, over and over. And he pushes his glasses up his nose more times than he needs to. He's not entirely comfortable in his own skin, that's pretty clear, but it's sort of adorable, because he has every reason to be. He definitely knows a lot about lighting. I haven't done anything but nod and make some encouraging noises, and he's going on and on, getting really excited about the topic, like he's thrilled someone wants to know about it.

"So," I cut him off. "How do you like the show? Taylor's really great as Sarah, right?"

He immediately blushes. "She's . . . she's incredible."

I grin. "You like her?"

He rears back like he's afraid I'm teasing him, but I just keep smiling so he knows I'm on his side. Then he relaxes . . . but he's still blushing.

"I don't really know her. We've said maybe two words to each other."

"Really? But you're both doing the play. All Tee talks about is this play and how incredible everyone is, and—"

Alarm in his eyes again. "'Tee'? You're her friend?"

I nod. "She's a really good friend of mine. But don't freak out. I'm not going to embarrass you or anything. I just don't get it. You seem like you like her . . . so talk to her. She's really nice. And I bet she'd like you. You're cute. Wait a minute—how tall are you? Are you over six feet?"

"Um . . . six feet exactly."

"Okay, good . . . and you're an upperclassman? Junior or senior?"

"I'm a senior."

"Good! Good! Then yes, you should go after her. What's your name?"

"Leo."

"Nice to meet you, Leo. I'm Autumn."

Leo smiles, and I'm elated because I have found the clear answer to Taylor's problems. Why pine after a boy who may-or-may-not-be-but-probably-is impossible to get when there's a perfectly good, perfectly cute, perfectly *interested* boy right here! Yes, he's a little skittish, but he just needs some work. He's like the stray puppies my mom finds for her rescue shelter. They're nervous at first, and you have to be very gentle and patient. But when you are, after a while you're rewarded with a prize of a pet.

I chat Leo up for a bit while we wait for the actors' notes to finish. He doesn't have a lot to say beyond the topic of stage lighting, but I'm guessing that's because that's where his head goes when he's in a theater. Plus, he's kind of on the clock, I guess.

When notes are done, Taylor runs up the aisle to meet me. She's holding Ryan's hand and the two are practically skipping they're so elated after the run-through. Leo gets up to move when he sees them coming, but I tell him to stay.

"Autumn!" Taylor cries. "What did you think? Did you like it?"

"I loved it," I say honestly. "You're incredible. And *you*," I add to Ryan, "I mean . . . wow."

For just a second Ryan becomes that smoldering bad

boy. "Thanks." He turns to Taylor and adds, "Your friend's got taste." Then he drops the attitude and gets giddy again. "Tee, seriously? You saved me in our dance. I don't know how you led while you were following, but you totally did. If this was a performance, I'd owe you my life."

"Whatever. I did nothing. You're brilliant. And I'm officially introducing you to Autumn. Autumn, Ryan, aka my boyfriend, Sky."

"A boyfriend who's about to prove his worth by taking his best girl to the fabulous Aventura Mall food court," Ryan says, then asks, "Want to join?"

"I can't. I have homework," I say. "You guys both know Leo, right?"

"Sound guy?" Ryan asks.

"Lighting."

They all say their hellos and then there's silence as I wait for Leo to say something charming, interesting, or in any way at all conversation-continuing.

"I gotta go" is what he comes up with. And he follows that with "See you next rehearsal."

"Nice guy, right?" I say brightly. "Super chatty. We were having the most amazing conversation during your notes—"

"I told you," Taylor says, "everyone with the play is incredible. It's a phenomenal group."

"*You're* phenomenal," Ryan corrects her. "I prefer to think of myself as more . . . *majestic.*"

"Shall we head to our fabulous mall date, Your Majesty?" Taylor asks.

"Most assuredly, my darling," he says, then asks me, "Sure you don't want to come?"

I tell him I am sure, but I don't tell him the other thing I'm sure about, which is that I have some serious work cut out for me if I'm going to bring peace and harmony to Taylor by getting her together with Leo. I try to find the guy and talk to him, but he's gone, probably tucked away with the lights somewhere. I'd use the map to get to him, but those lights are awfully high above the stage. If he is up there and I join him, there's a ridiculously good chance I'll plummet to my painful death. Better not risk it. Instead I go home and plow through a couple pages of *Les Misérables,* which is already making me so *misérable* that even visions of Hugh Jackman aren't helping. I switch to Algebra 2, which is just as cruel. It's math *and* letters. The creator clearly had it out for dyslexics. I can only handle a couple minutes of that before I go to history. That I enjoy—we have a really interesting textbook that makes U.S. history read more like a novel than a class—but it's still a lot of reading, pretty dense with information, and it takes a long time to get through each page. I keep going with it after dinner, but when I can't bear to do any more afterward, I realize I have an out. I text Jenna. She's home in her room for the night, so I hurl my books into a backpack and pop over to her place. Studying's a million times easier when she and I do it together over cheese curls and Diet Coke. At least that's my snack. Jenna opts for sugar snap peas, hummus, and water, because she's a runner and there's clearly something seriously wrong with her taste buds.

The next day I'm back on my Taylor/Leo mission. J.J. drives me to school and I put my books in my locker just like always, but instead of hanging with my friends on the lawn before class starts, I slip into an empty classroom and I write Leo's name on the map.

I appear across the school, immediately outside the boys' bathroom, so close to the door that Leo practically slams into me when he walks out.

"Hi!" I say.

He screams.

I link my arm through his and steer him toward an inconspicuous corner. Class is starting soon and I don't have time to dawdle. "So yesterday. I know you like Taylor, but I noticed you didn't really talk to her."

He pushes up his glasses and looks down at his shoes. "She makes me nervous," he admits. "I never know what to say to her."

"Say anything!" I tell him. "You see her every day at rehearsal, right? Just jump in and say anything."

"It's hard," he says. "She's always with the other actors. Especially Ryan."

"Forget Ryan," I say. "He is not an obstacle."

He looks pained. This might be a lost cause.

"I'm trying to help you here," I tell him, "but if you don't like her enough to go after her . . ."

I start to walk away, but he quickly grabs my arm and stops me, just like I hoped he would.

"No, I do," he insists. "I'm just . . . I'm not good at this kind of thing."

"But now you are because you've got me in your corner. Tell you what," I say, getting an idea, "I think you just need a different environment. The theater's hard. She's onstage, you're behind it, right?"

"Kind of above and in front of it, but yeah."

"So we get you away from there. My friend Reenzie's having a Halloween party Saturday night. Taylor will be there. So will you."

"Reenzie . . . *Tresca*?"

Leo pales. Now that we're friends, I sometimes forget Reenzie is still the awe-inspiring It Girl of Aventura High.

"I don't think she'd want me at her party," Leo says, "and she's not so nice to people she doesn't want around. *You* know that, I know."

I also forget that while most people at my school have very short memories, some do remember the hell Reenzie put me through last year. Some also think *I* was the one at fault and putting people through hell, but they're mistaken. Generally I'm happier with the people who've moved on to the next shiny thing and forget any of it ever happened. Just makes life easier.

"She'll be fine," I say. "I'm inviting you. Plus, you'll be in costume, so you won't stand out. Wear a *Phantom* costume. It's Taylor's favorite musical. You'll blow her mind."

"A phantom?" he asks. "Like a ghost costume?"

"*Phantom*," I say. "*Phantom of the Opera*. Just do it. Trust me."

I actually don't really care if he trusts me, I just need him to listen. It's class time after that, so I have to run. I consider making him give me his phone number so I can check his progress, but then I imagine Taylor flipping through his texts once they're together and seeing how I helped arrange everything. I'm not sure she'd appreciate it. I'll just have to pop in on him . . . which I do Friday night. Taylor, J.J., Jack, Reenzie, Amalita, and I all go to the away game to cheer on Sean and basically drive Ames to her date with Denny McNack. I excuse myself at one point and walk out to a tucked-away corner, where I write "*Leo*" on the map.

Suddenly I'm in his bedroom, standing in a pile of dirty laundry right next to his unmade bed. The room is a disaster of books, clothes, and papers. Leo's diagonally in front of me, sitting at his desk and completely concentrating on Internet chess, so he doesn't see me.

I'm about to tiptoe out of the room, scurry out his front door, and ring his doorbell, when I notice a bag on his bed. It's from a costume store. I edge closer. I have to peek.

The bag is closed, so I lift it open the teeniest bit. . . .

It crinkles so loudly, Leo spins around. I hit the deck and roll under the bed just in time.

"Is someone there?" Leo's voice is nervous, but I don't stick around to hear more of it. I saw what I needed to see.

Inside the bag is a *Phantom of the Opera* costume. Leo's a diligent pupil. My superhero powers remain strong. Before he can get any closer to my hiding spot, I write the name of the football stadium on the map and blink away.

I appear on the deck of a giant boat, and a couple locked in a heated kiss looks very confused when they suddenly notice me only two feet away from them.

"Great cruise," I say. "I love this liner."

Then I run until I'm beyond their sight and write the stadium name on the map again, correctly this time.

"What took you so long?" Taylor asks when I get back to my seat. "Denny just scored a touchdown!"

"And what did he do after?" Amalita asks.

Taylor smiles. "Held up the football, then pointed it right at Ames."

"Only the beginning," Ames says. "By Reenzie's party tomorrow, we'll be in matching costumes."

"Gag me," Jack says.

"It can be done tastefully." J.J. glances at me when he says it. He's heard my Halloween stories. I smile.

"You only say that because you got roped into matching Carrie Amernick's," Reenzie says.

"You and Carrie are on again?" I ask J.J. "How did I not know this?"

"Because we're not," he says. "She got me to tell her my costume, and now she says she's going to match it."

"Total waste," Jack clucks. "I offered her the chance to be D.C. comic royalty, Batman and Catwoman."

"Give it up," Ames tells Jack. "Carrie is not now, nor has she ever been, into you."

"You also shouldn't be so desperate for J.J.'s sloppy seconds," Reenzie says. "It's a little pathetic."

"Pathetic meaning you think I can do better?" Jack asks. "Are you saying *you* want to be my Catwoman?"

"I am two seconds away from scratching your eyes out for even suggesting such a thing," Reenzie says.

"Totally cool with that," Jack says.

Our team ends up winning the game; then we all wait around afterward until Sean and Denny are both showered and out. We're all planning to grab some food at a diner nearby that J.J. Yelped, and Sean invites Denny and Ames to come along . . . which nearly gets him slaughtered by Ames. She's safe, though—Denny says he already has other plans for them.

The rest of us go out and we're seated in one of those semicircle booths. I can see Reenzie jockeying to get next to Sean, but I manage to signal J.J., who is a true friend and gets it. He wraps her up in complete nonsense questions about the party tomorrow night, and by the time they're done, Sean is snugly ensconced between myself and Taylor, with me on the end and Jack on Taylor's other side, so Reenzie can't even get close. The restaurant is cheap, greasy, and loud, so it's impossible to talk to anyone except the person right next to you. Perfect.

"Halloween tomorrow," Sean says, leaning close. "You okay?"

I'd told him about my whole Halloween tradition too. "Sort of. I mean, it's good we're all hanging out. That makes it a little better. Thanks for asking."

"If it helps take your mind off it, you can just concentrate on other things . . . like how valiantly I led our team to victory tonight."

"You mean how humbly?"

"Absolutely," he says. "I'm always humble."

"That's good . . . 'cause I'm pretty sure it wasn't *your* butt I saw running into the finish area four times."

"*End zone,*" he says. "And are you really just watching our butts when we run?"

"I'm not the one who put you guys in tights," I say. "Nor am I the one who called it the *end zone.*"

We spend the entire late-night-breakfast chatting as if we're the only ones at the table. And even though the booth is big enough to give us all a little personal space, he keeps his side pressed against mine. It's like Sean's body has already decided we're back together. I just need his head to get the message.

Tomorrow at Reenzie's party. I already have it set up for Ames and Taylor. Now I just need Sean to come through and we'll all have the peace and harmony we deserve.

8

My phone beeps. It's a tweet that mentions me. From @CatchesFalls, which is my mom.

@AutumnFalls, Happy #H-ahhhh-lloween!

Attached is a picture of her at the spa, wearing a white robe and a white towel-turban, lying back in a chaise, cucumbers over her eyes.

There are a million things wrong with this, and I'm not even talking about the obvious fact that this is not how we celebrate Halloween. I know she thinks the "ahhhh" in her H-ahhhh-lloween is supposed to be like a relaxed sigh, but everyone will think it's a scream. Then there's the fact that you can't use dashes in hashtags. And that even if there were no dashes, #H-ahhhh-lloween is way too cheesy to trend, so it does *not* merit a hashtag. Finally there's the picture, which isn't something I feel like the world needs to see.

Basically, what I'm saying is that for their own protection, moms should not be allowed near social networking. They only embarrass themselves.

I love my mom, though, so I tweet back: @CatchesFalls— love it! #H-ahhhhh-lloween!

See, I even used her dorky hashtag. That's how supportive I am.

I'm glad I'm going out tonight. Erick is already gone, and obviously Mom's away. The house is completely empty of Halloween decorations, and I've left all the lights out except the one I'm using in my room so trick-or-treaters don't even dream of coming by. We don't have any candy in the house. If I weren't bugging out of here, I'd be totally depressed.

Sean and I getting back together tonight would be the perfect way to turn around Halloween and make it good again.

It's dark out but still early in the evening when my doorbell rings. Taylor, Sean, Ames, J.J., Jack, and I are required to get to Reenzie's an hour before the party officially starts so that when other people start showing up, it'll seem like it's already in full swing. Sean lives right next door to her, and Ames said she'd go with Denny, but the rest of us are driving together in J.J.'s car.

I'm spending the night at Taylor's, so I grab my duffel bag, then check myself in the mirror one last time. Blood-shot contacts, dark eye circles, rat's-nest hair, railroad-track scars, a little blood trickling down my chin, tattered white dress.

I like it. I look hideous and kind of great at the same time. I hope Sean thinks so too.

I run downstairs and throw open the door to find J.J. in a very proper dark suit complete with vest and bow tie. His eyes and cheeks are gray and sunken, and his hair is pitch black. He holds a cloth napkin over one arm and a domed silver tray in the other hand.

"Vampire butler, at my service?" I ask.

He gives me a dangerous smile, revealing sharp white fangs. "Indeed. Perhaps a snack for the zombie bride?" He lifts the dome on his tray and shows me a human brain. A plastic one. I assume.

"My favorite," I say. "You always know the right thing to bring. Shall we?"

"As you wish."

He gives me his non-tray arm and walks me to his car, where I manage to slip off my shoes and get my feet on the dash even in costume, which I feel is no small accomplishment. On our way to Jack's and Taylor's, J.J. anagrams our costumes. I'm "imbibed zero," which seems like a smart plan for the party, while he is a "veritable rump," to which I respond that I'll take his word for it.

Taylor went girly this year. She's the Tooth Fairy, and she has to take off her wings and slide them into the trunk before she can fit into the car. She's a cloud of pink and sparkle, and all I can think is how Leo will lose his mind when he sees her.

Jack's wearing a leather jacket, jeans, and a T-shirt.

"What about your costume?" I ask him. "I thought you were going to be Batman."

"That was only if I had a Catwoman," he says. "Without that, I went cooler. I'm Star-Lord, from *Guardians of the Galaxy*."

"When you say 'cooler,'" J.J. asks, "to what exactly are you comparing it?"

"Hey, watch it," Jack snaps. "Star-Lord is unbelievably cool."

"And you say 'unbelievably' because I totally don't believe it?" J.J. asks.

"Just wait," Jack says. "Girls will be dying for me tonight."

"Because you're planning to poison them?" J.J. asks.

I break it up to ask for anagrams for the Tooth Fairy ("Thy Tooth Afire") and for Jack's costume ("'Ill Partner Leg'—you wanted an anagram for 'Girl Repellent,' right?"), and soon we're at Reenzie's house.

I get a little heartsick when I see it from the outside. My dad would have loved it. It's illuminated by just enough well-placed, eerie lights to show off the cobwebs draped over every surface. Ghoulish jack-o'-lanterns flicker from the porch and are scattered over the lawn, and electric eyes peer out from the bushes and trees. Wails and screams tickle the edge of my hearing, so soft I almost think my ears are playing tricks on me. Then, when we're halfway up the walk to Reenzie's door, a coffin pops open and a skeleton bolts upright. Jack screams.

"That was in character," Jack says when he recovers. "Star-Lord would totally scream at that."

"Right," J.J. says. "Because he's so cool."

Inside the place is even better. The party is in Reenzie's basement, which has been transformed into a combination of crypt and dance club. Black lights give everything an unearthly glow, music pounds through the room, and a fog machine pours a layer of gloom over the floor.

Reenzie's dressed as a mermaid, with blue and green eye shadow and sparkles all over the parts of her body not covered by her seashell halter top and tail-skirt. Her hair extensions are braided with green and blue "seaweed" and hang down below her rear end.

No shock—she looks disturbingly gorgeous.

While she works on the music, making sure she has the right playlist going, Sean's on his hands and knees adjusting the fog machine.

"What was that you were saying last night about the end zone?" I ask.

"Hey!" He quickly jumps up. Then when he sees me, something happens to his smile. It changes. All of a sudden, it means something else. "Wow. You look . . . fantastic."

Pretty sure my whole body smiles. This is *exactly* what I wanted to happen tonight. "Thanks," I say. "You look . . . not in costume."

Sean's wearing his football uniform.

"Not true," he says, his eyes locked on mine. "This uniform is my brother's, from college. That makes it a costume."

I shake my head. "Demerits for lack of creativity. You could have at least splashed some blood on it, tossed a set of fangs in your mouth. . . . Haven't you ever seen the movie *Beetlejuice*? There's a whole dead football team in it. You easily could have been one of them."

"You're saying I failed Halloween."

"Horribly. Hopelessly."

He keeps moving a little closer and a little closer as we talk. Now he's so close I can feel the space between us. It's electric.

He reaches out and runs his finger along the scar on my cheek. "*You're* really good at it. The party hasn't started yet. Maybe you could help me fix my costume."

Is he saying what I hope he's saying?

"Autumn!" Reenzie screeches. She races over with the teeny steps her tail allows her. "Where's your veil?"

"I don't have one," I say.

"You're a zombie *bride*," Reenzie says. "You need a veil. Go up to my room. Tall dresser against the wall by the window. All costume stuff. I was Corpse Bride a few years ago; you'll find a veil."

"Really?" I feel a little nauseous at the idea, and not just because I don't want to break up whatever's going on with Sean. Reenzie and I are friends and we hang out and all, but I haven't been in her room since last spring . . . when I snuck in and Sean caught me trying to steal files from her computer. That makes me sound evil, I know, but I swear I had a good reason.

Obviously I would never do anything like that now, but I still feel weird going up to her room.

"I'll go with you," Sean says, and I don't know if it's because he wants to be alone with me or because he's thinking about the last time too and is suddenly worried I'll do something bad.

"No way," Reenzie says. "I need you to keep working on the fog machine. Everyone else will be here soon." Then she looks at me. "You remember where my room is, right?"

Is that a dig? "Reenzie, I . . ."

She rolls her eyes. "Get over it. *I'm* over it. Just go."

There's no denying Reenzie. She gives me a shove to send me on my way, then assigns everyone else jobs that they have to do immediately, before the crowds show up, so I'm on my own.

I *do* remember where it is. As I trot up one flight of stairs, down the hall, then up another, I wonder if even a little bit of Reenzie's generosity has to do with improving my costume—or if it's a hundred percent getting me away from Sean.

My guess is a hundred percent getting me away from Sean.

Whatever. I'll find the veil quickly, then go back.

I get into Reenzie's room and immediately see the tall

dresser she was talking about, but something else catches my eye before I get there.

Her computer . . . which I know is the last thing I should be looking at after what happened last time, but this time I think Reenzie would approve. I'm looking because I see *myself* bouncing by on the screen.

Reenzie's screen saver is a slideshow from her iPhoto—the images float around and change after a little while. Right now the one bobbing by is a selfie Reenzie took of the two of us. It's from a football game—the first of the season, I think. I remember I was still shocked that we were hanging out together, but even more amazed that we genuinely kind of clicked.

I shouldn't have been that surprised, I guess. Even during the worst of last year, we bizarrely had some good times together. Granted, I was in the middle of an evil scheme at the time, but hey, it all worked out for the best.

I watch the screen saver for a little while more—it's all pictures from this year: the beach, the football games, hanging on the lawn at lunch, the mall . . . goofy stuff.

And just a year ago my entire life was falling apart. I guess I've come a long way.

I'm about to go get the veil when I see another picture float by. A picture of Sean grinning next to a statue of an enormous green man dressed in a leafy toga.

My heart stops.

I know that picture.

I pull out my phone and scroll to my cache of photos,

the ones Sean sent me from his summer tour of the U.S. "because he was thinking of me."

The picture of him with the Jolly Green Giant on Reenzie's computer screen? It's the same one he sent me.

I keep staring as all the familiar images pop up: Sean with the sock monkey statue, with the giant beagle-shaped inn . . . they're all the same as mine.

Did he send her the same texts too? Did he say he knew she'd appreciate each picture? Did he say he was really looking forward to seeing her when he got back home?

Is he asking *her* if she'll help him fix his costume now that I'm upstairs? Before we all got here to the party, was he sitting pressed up next to her the way he was sitting with me last night?

The room is spinning. I have to get out of here.

I rummage through the tall dresser. Reenzie wasn't lying—it's crammed with all kinds of costume pieces: masks, capes, sashes, bloomers, and eye patches . . . the kind of thing I'd normally want to pick through so I could start planning next year's Halloween costume now, but all I want to do is grab the veil and get out before those pictures cycle around and come back on Reenzie's screen.

The veil's in the last drawer I search. I grab it and run down to the basement. I was gone long enough that the party's in full swing now. Music blares, and a stew of conversation buzzes through the room. Lights strobe, and with the sprawling basement full of people in costume, it's hard to see who's where.

Reenzie finds me, though. I hear her voice behind me. "Good, you've got it!" She takes the veil and fixes it in my hair.

"I noticed your screen saver," I say. I try to keep my voice light and casual. "Cute pictures!"

"Aren't they? They're all from this year."

"And the summer, right?" I dig. "I saw some of Sean . . . from his football camp trip?"

Reenzie spins me around to check the veil from the front. As she checks it, she smiles. "Yeah. It was nice. Our parents are so close, we've always spent the summer together. This was the first one we didn't. It felt a little weird, but he texted me every day and sent me goofy pictures. . . . It was like we were still hanging out even when we weren't."

"Every day?" I ask. My voice is shaky now, but the room is loud. That has to hide it. Sean did *not* text me every day. Close, but not every day.

"Almost," she says. Then she gives the veil a final tweak. "There. You look beyond." She links her arm in mine and leans in close, like she's telling me a sisterly secret. "I actually think it was good we weren't around each other all summer. He never had the chance to miss me before. I think it made him appreciate what we have. And since he came back, things have been . . . different. I feel like it's only a matter of time now . . . you know?"

Oh, I know. I know because I feel the same way about Sean and *me*.

At least, I felt that way until tonight.

9

I want to talk to Sean, but the party's not the place. There are too many people, and he's always in the middle of some group. Or when he's not, Reenzie has him running around helping with the snacks or the music or the fog machine.

So since I can't do anything to make my life more peaceful and harmonious at the moment, I figure I can at least help my friends.

Now I just have to find them. I know Taylor is somewhere, since she came in with us, but I haven't seen Amalita at all. That doesn't mean much, though. It's a crowded party.

"Hey," I ask Jack when I find him chowing on a jack-o'-lantern-shaped cupcake. "Have you seen Ames?"

"I don't think she's here," he says. "Haven't seen her. She really should just get a room."

He isn't making sense. "Who, Ames?"

"No, Carrie."

He nods to the makeshift dance floor, where Carrie Amernick, ridiculously pushed up and pinched into an over-sexy French maid outfit, is basically painting herself all over Alec Hoeffner, one of the football players.

"I thought she was dressing to match J.J.," I say.

That's when Carrie opens her mouth in a leer that shows off her vampire fangs.

"Well, there we go," I say. Then I wince. I'm a little embarrassed for her, actually, because even though she's slathering her body on Alec's, she's staring at J.J. like she wants him for lunch. He seems oblivious, dancing in a group with—oh, there she is—Taylor, Ryan (who's dressed as Elvis), and a few other actors from the play.

"Want to know the sick part?" Jack asks.

"That she's only dancing like that to get J.J.'s attention?"

"No, that if she wanted to slime on someone, she could totally have used me. I've been right here the whole time."

I just look at him.

"What?" he asks. "I can't have her, so I want her more. Everyone's like that."

I want to tell him he's wrong, but maybe he isn't. It's got to be why Carrie's making an idiot out of herself over J.J. And why Ames was losing her mind until she got Denny's attention. And it's definitely why Taylor's so set on Ryan . . . but she won't be for long. I leave Jack and case the room until I find Leo. Not only did he make it in the correct costume, but he's also in character, lurking in the shadows and watching Taylor from afar.

At least, I think that's in character. I've never seen the musical. Even if it is in character, I'm pretty sure Leo isn't doing it on purpose. It's just who he is. I run up to him, a huge smile on my face. "Leo!" Then I peer closer. A white mask covers half his face and he's not wearing glasses. "It is Leo, right?"

"Yeah. Autumn?"

The one eye I can see well is squinting. "You're not wearing contacts?"

"I can't. I've tried, but the feel of something on my eyes . . . it makes me pass out. Even thinking about it . . ."

He reels and puts a hand on my shoulder to steady himself. "Easy," I say. "Focus on here. You look amazing. Has Taylor seen you?"

"I don't think so," he says.

"You haven't gone up to her?"

"No!" He says it quickly and scandalized, as if I'd asked if he'd set her on fire.

"Leo, you have to talk to her."

"How? What would I possibly say to a girl like her?"

"Talk to her about stuff you have in common. Like theater! Talk about theater."

"I don't know anything about theater," he says. "I know lights."

"Okay, then outside theater. What do you like to do?"

"I like chess a lot," he says. "I play it online all the time."

"Moving on," I say. "Outdoor stuff. You like the beach?"

"I peel."

"Forget things in common. You like her, right? You think she's pretty?"

He looks at her and the visible half of his face gets dreamy. "She's the most beautiful pink blur I've ever seen."

"Yes! Good, Leo! Go with that! But leave out the blur. Just tell her how beautiful she is. And here." I pull out my phone and look up *Phantom of the Opera.* "Prep. That's how you're dressed, so she'll want to talk about that. Pretend you're a huge fan. And tell her that from watching rehearsals, you think she's talented enough that she should go to an acting school for college. A conservatory?"

"Really?" he asks. "Aren't those limiting in terms of an overall liberal arts education?"

"That's on the list of what *not* to say. Tonight you are pro–acting school, pro-*Phantom,* and pro-anything-you-can-remember-about-her-*Guys-and-Dolls*-performance-to-compliment. And the beautiful thing. Got it?"

He nods. "Yeah, okay. Thanks, Autumn."

"No problem," I say. "That's what superheroes do."

"Are you a superhero?" he asks. "I thought you were a zombie bride."

"Just study," I say.

After Leo bones up on *Phantom,* I look for a moment to get Taylor away from Ryan. For a while it doesn't seem possible, especially when the two of them start theatrically tangoing across the basement floor. They're pressed cheek to cheek and she follows him effortlessly. When they move slightly apart and look into one another's eyes, I see sparks.

Was I wrong? Is Ryan actually interested in Taylor?

He dips her dramatically, and I see Taylor breathlessly lean upward for the kiss she knows is coming.

Instead he pulls her back to her feet, twirls her so she's facing away from him, then puts his hands on her hips and invites everyone to grab on for a conga line.

Mission back on track.

I pull Taylor off the conga line. She still looks shell-shocked from the kiss she didn't get. "Hey!" I say. "Check out the Phantom!"

I drag Taylor toward Leo. She lights up when she sees the costume. "You're the Phantom—I love it!"

"Thanks," Leo says. "Did you know they usually double-cast the role of Christine?"

"Yes! I *do* know that!" Taylor says. "Producers think it's too much for one actress to handle all the performances. Which is weird, because the Phantom's role is just as challenging. And audiences want to see the main actress."

"Exactly," Leo agrees. "I mean, imagine if someone came to *Guys and Dolls* and saw anyone but you playing Sarah. They'd miss out on the most incredible performance ever."

Taylor's melting. I can see it. As I start to slip away, I hear Leo clinch it with, "You look really beautiful in that costume. You look beautiful *every* day. Especially when you're onstage. Hey . . . have you ever thought about a conservatory for college?"

My work here is done. I'd say halfway done, but Ames isn't anywhere. I wonder if she got sick. Maybe it was

Denny who got sick, but that wouldn't be enough to keep Ames from Reenzie's party. Or maybe it would. Maybe she's scoring new-girlfriend points by bringing him chicken soup or keeping him company on FaceTime while he gets over a cold. Like I did with Sean when he called me from Michigan when he was getting over food poisoning and we watched *When Harry Met Sally . . .* together over the phone. It was funny because in the movie Harry and Sally watch movies together over the phone and neither of us said that it meant the two of us would go from being friends to being together just like the lead characters in the movie; it was totally implied.

At least I thought it was. Now I wonder if he called Reenzie right after he hung up with me. I wonder what movie they watched together over the phone.

No. Have to get Sean out of my head. Can't do anything about him right now. I grab Jack and pull him onto the dance floor with J.J., and the three of us jump around for the next couple hours until it gets really late and the party dwindles down to around twenty people, including myself, J.J., Reenzie, Sean, Jack, Taylor, and Leo.

Yes, Taylor and Leo, who talk almost constantly after I leave them to their own devices. I do notice Leo subtly checking his phone a couple times along the way, but I don't think Taylor sees, and I know he isn't doing it to talk to other people but to keep up his research. I like that. It shows dedication. Taylor deserves someone motivated to impress her.

Ryan's already gone. Carrie Amernick is sticking it out,

though Alec Hoeffner's trying very hard to pull her away for some serious one-on-one sliming. Poor guy doesn't realize it only counts for Carrie if it's in front of J.J. There are enough people around that it's still a party, but it's small enough that it would be very easy for me to pull Sean aside and maybe get a moment outside to talk.

Easy, except that every time I look at him I feel my heart shred. Especially when he peeks up from whatever else he's doing and smiles like I'm the only person in the room. I have to keep reminding myself he's probably doing the same thing to Reenzie, just not when I can see.

I don't want to confront him. I don't want to hear him admit that he likes us both, or can't decide. I don't want him to tell me that every moment I thought was special was just a foreshadowing or an echo of the same moment with another girl. I already know it's true, but it'll be a million times worse to hear him say it.

I have to, though. I have to know.

I'm about to go up to him, when Alec gets an idea that I guess he imagines will force Carrie into some alone time. "Seven Minutes in Heaven—who's in?"

"What are we, twelve?" Reenzie laughs.

"Next we'll do the Ouija board," another girl says.

"Then Light as a Feather, Stiff as a Board!" Taylor chimes in.

"Then board games?" J.J. asks. "I'm seeing a 'board' theme."

Jack shrugs. "I'd play Seven Minutes in Heaven."

"Gonna need more than just you and me, Star-Lord," Alec says.

Jack looks so happy Alec knows his costume that I think his Seven Minutes in Heaven have already begun.

"It *would* be fun," a girl in a firefighter dress giggles.

"Seriously?" asks her friend in a slinky catsuit. "I mean, it's not like we can just play. We need a pen, and paper, and a hat, and a closet or something. . . ."

"Pen and paper upstairs," Reenzie says. "Sean knows where. We'll use the fire hat. And closet under the stairs—half empty, carpeted, and nice."

She looks at Sean and raises an eyebrow, and he scrunches his face. "For real?"

Everyone laughs. Sean does too, but a second later he's running up the stairs and the firefighter's handing her hat to Reenzie and Taylor's throwing open the closet door to make sure it's acceptable.

When Sean comes back down, he's grinning. "I can't believe we're doing this."

None of us can—we're all cracking jokes about how middle school it is—but we're doing it anyway. Reenzie writes down everyone's names on the paper, then cuts the paper into small pieces, one name per piece, and tosses the pieces into the hat. As she holds the hat above her eye level and shakes it around, she says, "Rules are simple. Two names are picked out of the hat. Boy/boy, boy/girl, girl/girl, doesn't matter. Then the two people go into the closet. When the door closes, I start the timer on my phone. When the alarm goes off, we open the door, but not a second before. Until then, whatever happens in the closet, stays in the closet. Names are *not* taken out of rotation when they're picked, which means every single one of you could end up with Jack."

Moans, gagging noises, and laughter ring through the room. Jack bows deeply, then tells Reenzie, "Or *you* could end up with Jack." He waggles his eyebrows.

"Should that happen, the game is automatically over," she says. A few people protest, mainly Jack, but she just shrugs. "Not my fault, in the rule book." She swishes the hat around some more and holds it over Taylor's and Leo's heads. "Pick one each," she says.

Sean catches my eye and smiles. I break out in a sweat. What if he and I are picked? What if he tries to kiss me? Do I let him, or do I spend seven minutes talking to him about what he's pulling with me and Reenzie?

Sean winks. I start to melt into the floor.

Crap. There's no way I'll talk to him. If we're shut in a closet together and he tries to kiss me, I'll kiss him back, and it'll be amazing and wonderful and world-upending . . . until the seven minutes ends and I feel worse than ever because I still don't know if I'm the only one he wants to kiss.

Don't be my name, I think, concentrating on the hat. *Don't be my name.*

"Carrie Amernick!" Taylor reads her slip of paper.

Carrie grins, baring her fangs eagerly at J.J. He's not even looking her way.

"Um . . ." Leo squints at the piece of paper. "Leah . . . Donovan?"

That's the firefighter. "Darling!" she cries to Carrie, and the two grab hands and run into the closet, where they spend the next seven minutes making ridiculous noises to get everyone laughing. The next two names are Alec and Reenzie. Reenzie does a big fake-gasp when her name is called with Alec's. Alec looks elated, but the reaction I really want to see is Sean's. He's smiling along with everyone else, but I can see he's not happy. It's a fake smile. And he spends the next seven minutes listening intently for any noise from the closet, all the while anxiously tapping the fingers of one hand against his thigh pad.

Taylor and Leo get picked together next, which proves to me that wishes can come true even without magic diaries. Taylor looks thrilled about it, but Leo looks like he might vomit. I trust that's nerves and not a change of heart, so I catch his eye and give him a big encouraging smile. He smiles back and nods slightly, and by the time they make it across to the closet, he looks a lot more relaxed and confident. I send him mental telepathy to kiss her, and I send the universe mental telepathy to make him a decent kisser.

The game goes on, and it pretty quickly goes from people possibly making out to people trying to put on the best show for everyone else to hear. Alec and Jack do a whole radio play of ridiculous noises when they're in together, while Reenzie and Taylor stage a fake fight during their time. Sean goes in a couple times, but never with Reenzie, and I end up with Leo, which is great because I get to hear that he did indeed kiss Taylor and it went well. Plus, I give him some more ideas about things to say to her, since he feels like he's running out. I even punch my cell phone number into his contacts in case he ever needs my help, though I warn him to delete any conversations we have right away so Taylor doesn't see them.

After a while the game winds down, but Reenzie's not quite ready to give it up. "One more! One more!" she shouts. I think she's hoping she'll get picked to go in with Sean. Carrie Amernick and Taylor agree, I'm guessing because Carrie wants to go in with J.J. and Taylor wouldn't mind going back in with Leo. Reenzie has Sean pick the name from the hat.

"J.J. Austin . . . ," he says.

Carrie hoots out loud. Sean reaches back into the hat. He pulls out another piece of paper, then gives me a knowing look and half-grin. "And Autumn Falls."

I smile. This is perfect. I've barely gotten to hang out with J.J. at all tonight, and I'm dying to vent to him about what I saw in Reenzie's room.

He's standing closer to the closet than I am, so I walk his way and extend my arm. "Shall we?"

"As you wish," he says.

Carrie Amernick snaps her fangs at me as we pass her, and I'm pretty sure she actually growls, but I ignore it.

The minute the door clicks shut, I lean close to J.J. and

speak a mile a minute in a low voice no one outside will be able to hear. "Okay, so remember when Reenzie sent me up to her room to get the veil? So I go up there and I'm about to get the veil when I see this picture of me on her computer screen. A picture of me in Reenzie's room! So of course I stop and check it out. . . ."

I go on and on, telling him everything, speaking even faster the longer I go because I don't want to run out of time. Then, just as I get to how I'm questioning everything I thought was bringing Sean and me closer, even the *When Harry Met Sally* . . . talking-on-the-phone-and-watching-the-movie-while-he's-sick thing . . .

J.J. leans in and kisses me.

And I think I kiss him back . . . a little. I mean, it's almost hard not to when someone leans in and kisses you. Unless you're repulsed. Like if it was Jack, I'd pull away and yell at him, but this . . . it was nice, I guess, just . . . unexpected. And strange. I mean, outside of Jenna, J.J.'s my best friend. I tell him even more than I tell Amalita. He's practically family.

That's the thought that gets me to pull away. Gently, not like I'm grossed out, because I'm not, it's just . . .

"What was that?" I ask.

J.J.'s face is still barely an inch from mine. There's hardly any light in the closet, so I feel him more than I see him, even though we're not actually touching anymore.

"Are you really that surprised?" J.J. asks.

"Yes," I answer honestly.

I can make out a gentle smile on his face. His eyes are soft but intense as they look into mine. "Autumn, I've wanted to be with you since the day we met. You're incredible and smart and funny, and I've never liked being around anyone as much as I like being around you. You're also the most beautiful girl I've ever seen."

I laugh a little. "I've seen the girls you've seen, and I'm not."

"I don't lie to you, though," he says. "You know that."

I *do* know that. And I don't know if it's the way he's looking at me or the things he's saying, but I get a little fluttery in my stomach. I kind of want to kiss him again . . . but I kind of don't. I'm not sure. I mean . . . he's J.J. We're not like that.

"J.J.—" I start, but I'm glad when he cuts me off because I'm not at all sure where I'm going.

"I know you like Sean," he says, "but you deserve more than him. You deserve someone who knows how amazing you are and doesn't flop around thinking there could be someone better."

He's right, I know, and it feels so good hearing him say it. It also hurts because I can't help thinking it would be even better to hear *Sean* say the same thing.

"I don't know what to say," I murmur.

"I know you don't." J.J. smiles. "I think I know you pretty well. And maybe I'm an idiot to say this stuff, but you're worth the risk. I needed you to know how I feel. Like this."

He touches my cheek and moves in closer, and this time I'm prepared. I kiss him back fully this time, and while I can't lie and say my whole body explodes the way it did when Sean kissed me . . . it's really nice. And loving. I like it. Still . . .

"I'm totally crazy for you, Autumn," he says in a low whisper, so close we could practically still be kissing, "but I'm not that guy who waits around forever. Think about it, and if you want someone who really cares about you and gets you, I'm here."

He springs away from me exactly two seconds before Reenzie flings the door open, and covers so it seems like nothing was going on. He stands up, putting on a show for the crowd.

"OW!" he yells, rubbing his neck. "Autumn, *I'm* the one with the fangs. I'm supposed to do the biting."

Carrie immediately runs over to check his neck for actual tooth marks, while I try to come up with something equally goofy to say . . . but I have nothing. I'm too stunned.

J.J. likes me. He wants to be my boyfriend.

So what do I want to do about it?

10

I spend that night at Taylor's, but I don't tell her about what happened with J.J. It would be too weird. Plus, she's too busy raving about her "discovery" of Leo.

"It's so crazy," she gushes. "He's been around at every rehearsal, but it's like I never even noticed him until tonight."

"I guess some guys just need a party to shine," I say.

"I guess . . . Did I tell you he thought I should go to theater school? Just from watching me at rehearsals."

"He's perceptive," I say.

Taylor sighs and hugs her pillow to her chest. "And an amazing kisser."

Thank you, universe, I say silently. "What about Ryan?"

"Ryan is incredible," she says, "but I don't know . . . it just wasn't going anywhere." She sits up quickly, an idea just hitting her. "Do you think he really is gay?"

"Does it matter?"

She thinks a second.

"No. Even if I had a chance with Ryan, Leo's better. He just gets me, you know? And we have a ton in common. Did you know *Phantom* is his favorite musical too?"

I could eat this up all night. But after she falls asleep, I start thinking about J.J. again. I text Jenna to make sure she's home, double-check that Taylor really is asleep, then use the map to zip to Jenna's house. I tell her everything: Sean flirting with me, the pictures on Reenzie's computer, J.J.'s admission . . . everything.

"Okay, first—not even remotely surprised. J.J. has been your Duckie from minute one."

It's a *Pretty in Pink* reference. Jenna and I have seen the movie about a zillion times. "But Andie doesn't end up with Duckie," I say.

"Sure she does. About six months after the movie ends, when she realizes Blaine's a complete tool and Duckie's a million times better for her."

"Projecting much?"

"I wish. I dumped my Blaine, but I'm Duckieless. I'll have to live vicariously through you."

"I'd rather live it vicariously through you," I say. "I don't know what to do."

"Take your time. I know J.J. said he won't be around forever, but he's J.J. He will. If you want to be with him, that's great—just take the time to make sure you *really* want to be with him first. You don't want to break his heart just because you're curious."

"Of course not," I say . . . but the truth is, I *am* curious. What would it be like to go out with J.J.? I've never really thought about him that way, but if you ask Carrie Amernick, she'll tell you he's an incredible catch, and Carrie's beautiful and popular *and* she already went out with him, so she knows what kind of boyfriend he is.

But Jenna's right. Curiosity isn't enough.

I spend another couple hours with her, then map myself back to Taylor's to sleep. The next day, she and I realize neither of us ever heard back from Amalita about the party, so we call until we reach her. We put her on speakerphone.

"Hi, Taylor! Hi, Autumn!" she says. Her voice is cheery, but there's something a little weird about it. A little strained and proper, maybe? I can't really put my finger on it.

"Where were you last night?" Taylor asks her. "Are you okay?"

"Were you delivering him chicken soup and watching movies together over the phone?" I add.

"No, he's fine," Ames says. "We're fine. We just weren't up for a party last night."

"Not *up for it*?" Taylor echoes incredulously. "We've been talking about this party for weeks!"

"Yes, but Denny wasn't feeling like a high school party."

I look at Taylor. This is weird. "A 'high school party'?"

"Yeah, you know . . . he just didn't want to go," Ames says. "So we hung out, just us."

"Did you have fun?" I ask.

"Way more fun than I would've at a party," she says.

"I've got to go, though. We're watching the pregame show and I don't want to talk over it."

"The . . . *what*?!" I say. "You're speaking another language and it's not Spanish. What are you talking about?"

Ames laughs a fake laugh. "The NFL! It's Sunday. I came over to Denny's to watch."

"For real?" Taylor asks. "Do you need us to rescue you?"

"You're funny," Ames says. "I've got to go. See you tomorrow."

She clicks off. Taylor and I look at each other, stunned.

"She's lost her mind," I say.

Taylor shrugs. "She's in love."

"She must be," I say. She, in fact, has to be *really* in love to both miss Reenzie's party *and* sit around watching football. It's weird . . . but I quietly pat myself on the back for making her so happy.

By the time I get home from Taylor's, Mom and Erick are back from their trips. It's good to see them . . . until Mom starts in about driving lessons again. She already called the instructor she told me about and emailed me a schedule of potential start dates. I say I'll check them out, but I delete the email before I even read it. Maybe she'll forget.

The next day is Monday, and I'm nervous about seeing J.J. He hasn't texted or called since the party, and I'm worried he's waiting for an answer I don't have. I'm not even sure if he's going to pick me up for school, and I don't want to call and ask him.

Turns out I don't have to. He rolls up the same time as always. I'm nervous when I slide into his passenger seat. I don't even take off my shoes or put my feet up on his dashboard, and I don't mess with his radio the way I always do.

Halfway to school he says, "Five hundred sixty-five."

"What?"

"Anagrams for 'awkward silence.' So far. I'm still thinking of more."

I blush. "J.J. . . ."

"'Awkward license.' That one's the most obvious."

"I'm sorry . . ."

"'Awkward ice lens.' That one's a gimme too."

"I just don't know what to say," I admit. "That's not a no. It's really an 'I don't know.' And I don't want to say anything until I do know . . . you know?"

J.J. smiles. "I didn't say what I said to make us weird around each other. That's the last thing I want. If you need time to figure stuff out, that's cool. I get it."

"You're sure?" I say.

"I'd be a jerk to pressure you into anything you weren't sure about," J.J. says. "That's not how I want us to be. I'm here. I'm not going to pine at your doorstep and text you puppy-dog-eyed selfies, but I'm here."

"Sure you won't send me selfies of you with puppy-dog eyes?" I ask.

"Maybe one. But it'll be a really creepy one."

"Excellent. Totally holding you to that."

I slip off my shoes, lean back in my seat, toss my feet

on the dash, and switch the radio station. Life is good . . . until we get to school and can't find Ames anywhere.

"Seriously?" I ask Taylor and Jack as we hang by the lockers. "None of you have seen Amalita?"

"We saw her," Sean says as he and Reenzie walk toward us. "She's with Denny. They're on the side lawn."

"Why?" I ask. "Why doesn't she bring him here to hang with all of us?"

Reenzie gazes pointedly at Jack, J.J., and I, then says, "Really?"

"Oh, come on," Jack says. "We're totally lovable."

"Speaking of lovable . . . ," Taylor says. She waves to someone down the hall. "Leo! Hey, Leo!"

Leo spies us from down the hall and beams when he sees Taylor. He joins us and puts an arm around Taylor. She leans against him. "Miss me?"

"Yeah. Of course."

"What did you do last night?"

Leo shoots me a panicked look, and I know what he's thinking. He has no idea what he should say, and he's guessing the truth won't work. There's an odd silence between them, so I jump in to rehash Reenzie's party, which is a conversation I know she'll love. Soon we're all reliving every moment, and that keeps us talking until class starts.

It's a good save, but if I'm going to keep their relationship going, I need to give Leo some more advice. I can tell he thinks so too. As he peels off to his first-period class, he discreetly pulls out his phone and raises his eyebrows.

He's asking me to text him.

When I get to class, I slip out my phone and text him:

You need to talk?

PLEASE! he writes. As soon as you can! I don't want to blow this.

On it. When's good?

Between third and fourth periods. I'll be outside the theater room.

Done and done.

So right at the end of third I look for him. I'm outside the theater . . . but Leo isn't. He doesn't show. I wait as long as I can, but we only get a quick grace period between classes. I don't want to be late. I've had bad experiences being late to class.

Did I get the place wrong? Did he want to meet me someplace else? I'd check the text, but just like I told Leo he should erase texts from me, I've been erasing texts from him.

I must have gotten it wrong. I must have read it wrong. Reversed the letters as usual. Now he's waiting for me someplace else and if I don't get there soon, we'll both be late for class.

I duck behind a pillar, pull out the map, and write Leo's name on it. I expect to appear in the hall somewhere close to him.

Instead I'm suddenly surrounded by half-naked guys.

No. No-no-no-no-no. This is *not* happening.

I'm in the boys' locker room. I see lockers, benches . . .

and way too many guys in tighty-whities. Or gym shorts. Or towels.

I need to write myself out of here *immediately*. Even though miraculously no one saw me pop in, I have exactly a split second before someone does. I hit the deck behind a giant cloth laundry bin full of towels, then slither so I'm between the bin and wall. All I hear are guys' voices and some shoving and pushing. The air is too thick with sweat and my face is way too close to the floor.

This is so not okay. I want to write myself out of here, but I'm afraid to move a muscle. I will die if someone sees me.

I stay down, barely breathing, until all the sounds fade away. The room is empty. Everyone's either changed and in PE or showered and back to class.

Yes.

I take a deep, relieved breath . . . and instantly regret it. The air is way too dank for that. I jump up, push the laundry bin away, and run . . .

. . . straight into a guy in a towel.

"Autumn?"

I wince. It's painful to look up, but I do. I even manage a big smile. "Sean!"

I gasp. He's wearing nothing but a small towel. And he's wet from the shower. The water beads like ornaments on his muscles. I want to touch each bead and pop it on his skin, then watch the water trail down his body.

I really have to stop. This is *not* a romantic setting. At all. Not even remotely.

But wow, he looks good in a towel.

"What are you doing here?" he asks.

"That's an excellent question," I stall, trying not to get distracted by the fact that he's wearing *only a small towel.* There's nothing under his towel. And by that I mean he's just wearing a towel.

"Autumn?"

Oh no. I totally got distracted. It's his own fault. You can't have a body like his and expect it *not* to be distracting when shoved behind a towel. Somehow I have the where-withal to tuck the map behind my back, even though I'm sure the last thing he's wondering about is whatever I might have in my hands.

"I was . . . meeting someone." I wince.

"In the boys' locker room?"

"It's . . . complicated. Nothing weird, though. I swear."

Sean laughs out loud. It echoes gorgeously. "It's always something weird with you," he says. "That's what I like best."

Is he . . . flirting with me? In the middle of the stanky boys' locker room? I'm so thrown I giggle and try to lean enticingly against the nearest surface, but then I imagine what horrors could be *on* the nearest surface and trip a little bit trying to avoid it. Sean reaches out to catch me— *taking both hands off the towel*—but he has clearly mastered the art of the wrap-and-tuck because it stays in place.

His arms, however, are wrapped around me. He's hold-ing me much closer than he needs to if he just wanted to steady me. My heart threatens to thud through my chest, and my limbs are spaghetti.

He's tractor-beaming me in with those eyes. And his smile. "I've missed this," he says softly.

"Holding me in the boys' locker room while you're wearing a towel?" My voice quavers.

We both hear the footsteps coming from the direction of the gym. I jump out of his arms and scramble for the main door. "See you at lunch!" I hiss. "And maybe we just, y'know, keep this between us."

I don't wait to hear what he says; I just zoom out the door. I'm so late to my fourth-period class now that I may as well just skip it, so I slip outside and find a place to tuck myself away and I text Leo.

You blew me off! WHERE WERE YOU??? I write, which is technically the wrong question.

I know where he was—he was in the boys' locker room getting ready for PE. The real question is why was he there and not at the theater where he was supposed to be? Still, I think I get the point across. Part of me is so annoyed with him I'm ready to leave him on his own to blow it with Taylor, but the two of them are my project, and they're making Taylor happy. Her peace and happiness depends on them working out. I need to keep it going until Leo's ready to continue without my help. So as long as I have my phone and some time, I sit and text him some more ideas for things to say to Taylor. Then I remind him:

MEMORIZE THIS STUFF THEN ERASE THIS TEXT SO SHE DOESN'T EVER SEE IT!

Once I'm done, my mind drifts back to Sean in his towel.

Okay, I admit it, my mind never really drifted *away* from Sean in his towel.

But it's not just how amazing he looked in the towel. What I can't get out of my head is the way he made me feel. When J.J. kissed me at Reenzie's party, it felt nice. When Sean had his arms around me—even in a disgusting boys' locker room—it felt atomic.

J.J. told me I deserve someone who knows how amazing I am . . . but don't I also deserve atomic?

If it weren't for the Reenzie thing, it would be easy. I'd be all about Sean. But I can't figure out if he's real. He says he loves that I surprise him with random acts of weirdness and he misses his arms around me, but what if he tells Reenzie he loves that she *doesn't* surprise him because he knows her so well, and he misses his arms around her?

Okay, he doesn't miss that because they were never together and they seem to throw their arms around each other a lot, but the point's the same. He's giving the same signals to both of us.

If it were me and Taylor or Ames instead of Reenzie, I'd talk to her and we'd unite to confront Sean and make him tell us the truth, but that would never work with Reenzie. I need to talk to Sean alone.

Hey, I text him. Can we talk, just us? LMK.

I add, P.S. excellent choice in towelry.

11

Lunch that day has me squirming. It's not the food; it's that all my friends and I are sprawled on the lawn like always, but every time I look at Sean, I see him not in his shorts and T-shirt, but the way he looked in the locker room. And when that happens, I get sweaty, my breath comes faster, and it seems like I'm having a mild heatstroke. To avoid this, I barely look at him. If I meet his eyes, mine skitter away a second later.

I don't think J.J., Jack, Reenzie, or Taylor notices. Sean, however, totally does. He hasn't texted me back yet, but he won't take his eyes off me, and he looks highly amused by my squirming. He even makes it worse by bringing up the morning's incident in a million different ways, just to make me crazy.

"It's so hot out," he says, flexing his biceps as he stretches his arms high. "I feel like I could use a shower."

"You had PE," Reenzie says. "Didn't you already shower?"

"Did I?" he asks, looking right at me. "I guess I forgot."

"Has anyone seen Ames?" I ask, changing the subject.

"She texted me and said she's off campus with Denny for lunch," J.J. says.

"That's weird," Taylor says. "She didn't go to the Halloween party, she didn't hang with us this morning, and now she's not at lunch."

"She has a new boyfriend," I say. "She wants to hang out with him."

"So he can shower her with affection," Sean says.

I blush and squirm.

"You don't see Taylor choosing her new guy over us," Jack says.

"That's because he has sixth-period lunch," Taylor says. "Otherwise I totally would."

"Would you, though?" Reenzie asks. "Or would you bring him here to eat with us?"

"We're a good group," Sean says. "Excellent manners." He takes a napkin from his lunch tray and spreads it across his pelvis . . . so it looks like a towel. Then he smiles and raises his eyebrows at me.

I can't even look . . . or not look.

Lunch continues on this way. Reenzie takes off early for an AP study group, J.J. lists a million road trips he wants to take in his new car, Jack is all about some superhero show on TV that's apparently having an epic episode tonight,

Taylor tells us all about the play . . . and Sean makes me squirm. When we all split off to go to our sixth-period classes, he falls in step next to me.

"You left so fast," he says. "You really made a clean break of it."

"Shut up!" I say, smacking his arm.

He laughs. "I got your text. Yeah, let's talk."

"Great. Want to hit the food court after football practice?"

He shakes his head. "Play-offs start next week, so Coach is working us pretty hard. What about Saturday?"

"Food court Saturday?"

"I'll pick you up Saturday afternoon and we'll figure it out. Two o'clock?"

"Great."

We split off and I'm almost to class when I see Leo running my way.

"Hey!" he says. "I didn't blow you off, I promise. I wouldn't. I was there, outside the locker room. I waited as long as I could."

"Outside the locker room?" I ask. "You told me outside the *theater* room."

Leo scrunches his face. "'*Theater room?*' I wouldn't even say that. You must have read it wrong."

Not a shocker. I can't even push back on it. "I probably did," I admit. "But you got the stuff I wrote?"

"And deleted the text, just like you asked. Thanks, Autumn. Taylor's . . ." He shakes his head, unable to find the words. "I never in a million years thought I'd get someone like her to even notice me. To have her as a girlfriend . . . you're amazing."

Aw. That makes me feel really good.

"Just bring her peace and happiness," I say; then I continue to class on a cloud of joyful satisfaction. I realize I'm not so much a superhero as I am a fairy godmother, which is probably even better. Less spandex.

The rest of the week is pretty normal, though I keep my eye on Sean and Reenzie. I know about the pictures and texts he sent us both all summer, and I know Reenzie thinks the two of them are on the brink of coupledom, but I want to gather even more evidence so I can throw it in his face on Saturday and see what he does. Normally I'd analyze everything with J.J. each morning in the car, but now that he's waiting for me to decide about him and me as a couple, there's no way. Right now things are great and normal between us; they'd get ugly if I asked for his help getting another guy, especially a guy J.J. specifically said he doesn't think is good enough for me.

Taylor and Ames can't help either, because they're too caught up in their own relationships. I don't even see Ames all week. None of us does; she's always with Denny. He drives her to school, they have lunches off campus. . . . I barely even see her in the halls because the two of them stay tucked away until the last second whenever there's a break, and they zip off for football and cheerleading right after school. Ames and I don't have any classes together either, so it's like she's disappeared from my life. We do text, though, and she tells me she's over-the-moon happy, so that's all that matters.

Still, I'd be feeling pretty alone if I didn't have the map. I use it to visit Jenna every night. We hang out in her room, eat snacks, listen to music, do homework, and dissect everything that happened each day in both our lives. If Dad's gifts are all about bringing peace and harmony to my little corner of the world, the map hit it out of the park.

There's one other pet project of mine: I visit Century Acres every day to pop in on Eddy. I don't stay for long, just enough time to say hello and let Eddy know how much I love her and show her what a terrific granddaughter I am.

And . . . you know . . . to look for Kyler Leeds.

So, yes, I tend to show up there a little later in the afternoon, after I come home from school, shower, reapply makeup, product up my hair, and put on one of my most flattering outfits.

In other words, I show up after dinner, in old-people time.

Mrs. Rubenstein has apparently figured out how to outsmart Eddy, because she's always in the comfy chair. That means I know within the first second whether Kyler's there because he'd be with her, but I can't turn and leave right away because then she'll know what I'm doing.

"Hi, Mrs. Rubenstein," I chirp, a huge smile on my face. "You look wonderful today."

"You're dressed up," she grouses. "Pretty fancy just to visit your grandmother."

It goes down like that pretty much every time. I think she's on to me. She never tells me what Kyler's up to or if he was there or when he'll be there, and I don't ask. I never see him, though, so either he's out of town or he's visiting "Meemaw" while I'm at school. Hopefully not because he's specifically avoiding me.

Friday night is the last regular-season football game of the year, so I let Jenna know in advance that I won't pop over because I'll be out late. Reenzie, Taylor, Jack, J.J., and I all sit together at the stadium like always, only now Leo's with us too. I get the sense he knows as much about football as I do, because like me, he always reacts a half second or so after the crowd. Mainly he's there to hug and kiss Taylor after big plays and get popcorn for all of us, so I think he's a fantastic addition to the group. He joins us at the beach after the game, but he and Taylor disappear on some romantic walk and I don't see them after that.

What's harder to take is that Sean and Reenzie disappear too.

I don't see when exactly it happens. We're all at the Shack getting ice cream; then my friends and I end up melding in with this whole group of people who want to walk down the beach to a mini-golf place, which sounds goofy and fun, so we all go. Sean and Reenzie are with us when we start the walk, but by the time Jack, J.J., and I are lining up at hole number one, they're gone.

I don't play a very good game of mini-golf. I hit the ball too hard. I can't help it. I keep pretending it's Sean's smiling face, telling me about how much he missed me, then swooping Reenzie off to do who knows what on the beach at night. Hypocrite. By the time we get back to the cars, his is already gone, and I'm sure Reenzie's with him. They'll probably stay up all night at one of their houses, curled up on a couch watching movies, his arm around her until they fall asleep right there . . . then Sean will wake up just in time to roll out and come to my house, thinking he can do the same thing with me.

Gross.

I consider calling him to cancel our meeting, but I want to tell him face to face how slimy it is to string Reenzie and me along. I build a whole speech in my head. I go to bed Friday thinking about it. I dream about me delivering it, though in the dream I have seven arms and I'm purple. When I wake up, it's pounding in my head, and once Jenna's awake I even use the map to write myself to her and practice it on her. I pop home in time to get myself extra cute, because I know the hotter I look, the worse it'll be for Sean to get dropped.

I suit up for battle in simple-but-sexy-sweet: little camouflage shorts, little butter-yellow tank top, hair long and loose. When he rings the doorbell, I'm ready. I fling open the door with major attitude.

"Hey, Autumn," Sean says. "You look beautiful."

"Thanks." I say it like the compliment doesn't even affect me, though I do notice that Sean doesn't look like he just rolled off the couch with Reenzie. He looks clean and fresh and rested. And he smells good.

And he's holding flowers. Tulips. In a bunch of different colors.

"Here," he says. "These are for you."

"Thanks," I say again. But I say it gruffly, and I don't elaborate. I'm sticking with the one-syllable answers. I have a speech to deliver, and I'm not going to let some flowers and a clean, great smell throw me off. Still, I can't just toss the flowers down to die. I let Sean in while I go to the kitchen and dig out a vase.

"We could really just talk here," I say, concentrating on the flowers and not looking into his eyes. Easier to stay on task that way. "My mom's at work and Erick's at his friend Aaron's."

"Actually, I already made plans . . . if that's okay."

There's something almost shy in his voice that makes my heart flutter . . . until I remind myself that his "plans" included disappearing with Reenzie last night too.

"Sure," I say, but I don't let myself sound excited. When the flowers are all set up, I grab my bag and head out to his SUV, which after his summer road trip is held together with more duct tape than ever before. He won't tell me where we're going, just drives for fifteen minutes until we pull into this park area I've never been before. Lots of trees, giant rolling lawns, and a massive body of crystal blue water that branches off into little rivers that look like they run forever. Little kids run around on the grass, couples hold hands and walk their dogs . . . there's even an ice-cream truck playing a tingly tune.

If I weren't about to totally tell Sean off, I'd be seriously charmed. Especially since it's November. Last time I popped over to visit Jenna in Maryland, it snowed there. For sure there are advantages to Florida.

But Sean's not going to win me over with pretty scenery. Not when I know what he's really up to.

He stops the car and I turn in my seat to face him. "We need to talk."

"We will." He gets out, pulls a backpack out of the backseat, and slings it on, then opens my door and helps me out. I don't need his help and I remind myself I don't want his help, but it would be rude to completely blow him off, so I take his hand and let him help me down . . . but I whip my hand back the second I'm on the ground.

He leads the way as we walk, and even though I try to start my speech a few times, he always asks me to please wait. "We'll talk, I promise—just not yet."

We get to a little dock. It's empty, except for one blue-and-white pedal boat—one of those two-person boats you sit in and pedal like a bike. There's a park near my old house where Jenna and I used to rent boats like these. This one has the two seats up front, a little storage space behind that, and a small deck at the back of the boat.

"Sorry," the man at the counter says. "This is the only one left and it's reserved."

"I know," Sean says. "I reserved it." He pulls out his ID and a credit card. The guy looks it over, then leads us to the dock. As we climb into the boat and the guy unhooks it, I wish I'd worn a hat. I'm going to get seriously charred on the water without one. Or maybe not—I can't imagine we'll be out here very long once I tell Sean off.

I try to keep my head of steam, I really do, but the boat keeps rocking, and Sean pedals faster than my legs can keep up, so mine are spinning like a cartoon character's, and the boat is rocking and even the ducks look nervous for us . . . so I start laughing. Sean laughs too, and we're so concentrated on getting our legs in sync and moving the boat forward that there's no way I can talk to him about anything except what we're doing.

Sean stops pedaling when we get to the middle of the lake. The sun sparkles off the water. The shore seems forever away. There are other boats around, but they're not close. We're all alone in the middle of the water, and everything is beautiful. When I turn to look at Sean, he looks brighter and clearer too, like the day has outlined him in bold.

"Why did you stop?" I ask.

"The ducks are hungry."

He reaches for his backpack and pulls out a ziplock bag full of bread slices. He hands me a piece, and we toss the bits into the water. Ducks zoom over to us from everywhere, cruising through the water like mini-speedboats. They huddle around our boat quacking insistently, and we dole out the bread as quickly as we can. One brave duck even jumps on the back deck of the boat, and Sean laughs when I scream.

"There's too many!" I laugh. "We have to get away!"

We pedal out some more, farther into the lake and down one of its branches. The waterway isn't as wide here, and tree branches hang their leaves over us like a canopy. Sean stops pedaling again.

"Too much exercise for the star quarterback?" I ask.

"Not enough food for the star quarterback," he corrects me. "But I brought snacks."

He reaches into his backpack again and pulls out snap-seal containers of cheese, crackers, and olives.

I peek into the backpack. "What else do you have in there, a table and chairs?"

"Lemonade," he says, pulling out a screw-top bottle. "But no cups. We have to share." He unscrews the top and takes a swig, then hands it to me.

"Classy," I say, and take a swig myself.

"Star quarterbacks are totally known for their class," he says. "So . . . you said you wanted to talk."

I don't really. It's much nicer sitting in the pedal boat on this beautiful branch of a lake snacking with Sean and pretending he might be in love with me. But I know better. I can't quite bring myself to deliver my amazing speech that would kick him in the stomach. It's too nice being here with him; plus, I'll kind of need him to pedal me back to the dock afterward.

"It's no big deal," I play it off. "I just noticed you and Reenzie disappeared at the beach last night."

"Yeah," he says. "I had to talk to her about some things."

"Oh really?" I ask. "Anything . . . interesting?"

"Yeah," he says again. "I had to tell her this."

He leans over and kisses me, and everything else disappears into the place where our lips connect. I'm so swimmy I think I'm falling into the water. When he pulls away, I'm breathless, but I realize I need to clarify something.

"When you say you had to tell her that," I ask, "do you mean you had to tell her *that* or that you were going to do that with me?"

Sean's face is still just an inch from mine. When he talks, I feel his breath against my skin. "That I was going to do that with you."

"That you were going to do . . . *what* with me again?"

Sean smiles. He leans in and kisses me some more. This time I don't stop to ask any questions.

12

"You're sure you're okay with this?"

I'm in J.J.'s car on Monday and he's driving me to school. I gave him an out. I made him sit in front of the house with the car idling while I told him what happened with Sean and that Sean and I are officially together now. If J.J. wanted to, I wanted him to kick me out and drive to school alone.

He says he's okay, but I'm not positive he's telling the truth.

"You're sure?"

"As sure as I was the last six times you asked," J.J. says.

"Yeah, but that's the thing. I'm not sure you were really sure when you said you were sure."

"I'm sure."

"You're sure you're sure?"

"What do you want me to say? Is it what I hoped you'd tell me? No. Do I think it's insane that anyone would even consider Reenzie when he has a chance with you? Yes. Do I think that in and of itself should have been a dealbreaker for you when it comes to Sean? Yes."

"Okay, you seem to be having this conversation with yourself," I say.

"But do I think Sean's a good guy?" J.J. continues. "Yes. Do I think that if he makes you happy and you want to be with him that I should be in your corner? Yes."

"Thank you," I say.

"Do I think that the fact you chose Sean over me puts your character in question and makes you a little less appealing as a prospective girlfriend? Yes."

"Wait . . . what?"

"You want me to be okay with it, right?" J.J. asks. "That's one of the reasons I'm okay with it."

"Okay," I say. "I guess . . ."

"And do I think that when you're old and gray and thinking about your greatest regrets in life, you'll weep a little as you sadly tell your grandkids about 'J.J., the One Who Got Away'?"

"Now you're just purposely being annoying," I say.

"Yes." He grins.

So J.J. seems honestly okay with it, which is good because he's still one of my best friends and I'd freak out if things got weird between us. I do hyperventilate a little when we get to school and meet up with our group and Reenzie links her arm through mine.

"Walk with me," she says, and I have horrible visions of

her tying a cement block to my ankles and throwing me to the bottom of the swimming pool. As we walk off, I cast a nervous glance over my shoulder at Taylor, J.J., Sean, and Jack. I hope that if I die, they'll tell my family I love them.

"I feel really stupid," Reenzie admits when we get outside. "That stuff I told you at my party about Sean and I getting together . . . I completely misread him. I'm sorry."

I couldn't be more surprised if she'd turned into a giant walking duck. Okay, maybe a little more surprised. But just a little.

"You don't have to apologize at all!" I assure her. "You were telling the truth. It's what you thought. I'm just sorry . . . I mean . . . I don't want to hurt your feelings . . ."

". . . or risk my vengeance?" She smiles.

"Actually, weirdly, I wasn't even thinking of that," I say, and I'm stunned that it's true. "It's just . . . you're my friend. I feel bad."

"Don't. It's Sean. It's not like he's the love of my life. Him I'll find in college, but not until senior year, so we can move to the same city together but live in separate apartments while we do our early-twenties thing and see if it'll work. Probably it won't, but then we'll come back together for our five-year college reunion and realize we were totally meant for each other all along. You'll be one of my bridesmaids. Sean will be a groomsman. You won't still be together then—sorry—but you'll totally have a wedding fling."

The really amazing thing is I know she's not joking. She really has figured this all out.

Then she gasps and grabs my arm tightly. "Oh my God."

I follow her gaze. We're rarely around this side of the school in the morning, but apparently this is where Denny and Ames like to hang out before classes these days. They're sitting on a wood bench . . . or at least Amalita's sitting. Denny's on his back with his knees bent, feet on the bench, and his head lying in Ames's lap. They're talking in low, sweet voices as Ames runs one hand through Denny's hair.

That's all fine. It's couple stuff, whatever. That's not the thing that made Reenzie gasp.

What made her gasp is Ames.

Amalita Leibowitz is a girl who loves cosmetics. Cosmetics, as I found out the day she and I first met, are in fact her Thing. She can't make it through a day without buying some new item, even if it's just a tiny sampler lip gloss. She layers her skin in cleansers, toners, hydrators, sunscreens, concealers, finishers, foundations, glosses, blushes, liners, shadows, and mascaras, not like a preschooler playing dress-up but like Vincent van Gogh applying layer after layer of paint until he'd achieved a masterpiece.

Today Amalita is naked.

Oh, she's wearing clothes, but her face is without a stitch of makeup.

"I don't believe it," I gasp to Reenzie.

She strides over to them, still holding me firmly by the arm. I really don't trust her to say anything subtly, so I start things off. "Hey, Ames! Hi, Denny!"

Denny peers up at me and sneers. Not his fault—I forgot for a second how weird I was the first time he saw me. Then he takes in Reenzie and smiles. He gives me a retroactive friendly "Hey!" then adds, "And if it isn't Marina Tresca."

Everyone knows Reenzie. Even senior football stars who never hang out in the school unless they have to.

"What did you do to Ames?" Reenzie shoots back.

Yeah. The light touch isn't really Reenzie's thing.

"What are you talking about?" he says.

I expect Amalita to jump in and bite Reenzie's head off, probably in a long string of Spanish, but she doesn't.

"What is she talking about, baby?" Denny asks Ames.

"I don't know, baby," she replies.

"I'm gonna throw up, baby," Reenzie says to me.

I still can't believe what I heard. *"Baby?"* I echo.

"Amalita, come talk to us," Reenzie says.

"Hey, if you have a problem with my girl Amalita, you can take it up with me," Denny says.

I laugh out loud. Like Ames would ever let anyone else fight her battles. But she just sits there, still petting Denny's head.

"Where's your face?" Reenzie asks Ames.

"Unless you've gone blind, you're looking at it, Reenzie," Ames says.

"You're not wearing any makeup," I say.

"I told her I don't like her with makeup," Denny says. "She's beautiful the way she is."

He leans up and he and Amalita kiss; then Ames looks at Reenzie and me with smug satisfaction.

Now, here's the thing. I'm all for women not wearing makeup. Those pictures on the Internet of celebrities without makeup—Gwyneth Paltrow, Rihanna, Drew Barrymore—they're beautiful without any makeup at all. No one *needs* makeup to be beautiful, and Ames doesn't either. Denny's totally right. She's gorgeous without any makeup at all.

But she's not Amalita. And I'm all for people reinventing themselves too, so if this is her New Thing, great.

It's just so not her personality . . . I don't know . . .

"And why aren't you wearing any jewelry?" Reenzie asks. "And what are you wearing?"

"Why are you such a *culito*?" Ames shoots back, but I'm only just realizing that Reenzie's right. Ames isn't wearing a single bangle—no earrings, no rings, no necklaces. She could get off that bench right now and she wouldn't even jangle, which is unheard of. Ames is usually a walking symphony. And she always dresses to accentuate her curves, in tight-but-flattering dresses or tailored tops and shorts . . . but today—it's hard to tell because she's sitting with Denny on her lap—it looks like she's wearing olive flouncy capris and a big white peasant top. Cute, for sure, but way more conservative than her usual style.

The bell rings for class. Denny gets up and Ames does the same. She barely comes up to his chest. When he wraps his arm around her, it's like he's cuddling a doll.

"I'm not going to fight with you," he says to Reenzie, "but I'm not going to let anyone talk to my girlfriend that way. Just watch yourself."

They walk off. Ames doesn't even look back at us, but she's all we talk about when the whole group of us is back together, sprawled on the lawn for lunch.

"I've been telling her for years she doesn't need makeup," J.J. says. "How come she never listened to me?"

"You really need us to answer that?" Reenzie asks.

"You'd look beautiful without any makeup," Sean says. He's lying on his side and I'm leaning against him.

"Aw, that's sweet," I say, and give him a quick kiss. "But you're not touching my lip gloss or mascara."

"And that is the proper answer," Reenzie declares.

"I think girls are way hotter without makeup," Jack says.

"You just insulted every girl here," Taylor says. "Autumn, Reenzie, and I are all wearing makeup."

"How is that an insult?" Jack balks. "I said you'd look hot without putting crap on your face."

"I had your back until 'crap on your face,'" J.J. says. "You always find a way to mess it up."

"The makeup isn't the point, though," I say. "She stopped wearing it because Denny said he doesn't like it on her."

"Right," Taylor says. "Denny should like her the way she is: the makeup, the bracelets, the dresses . . . whoever she is, that's who he should like."

"Because none of you have ever changed in any way for a guy," J.J. says drily.

"Never," Reenzie says.

"No!" I agree. "You shouldn't have to."

"You're really gonna make me do this?" J.J. asks. "Autumn, how many football games did you go to before you liked Sean?"

I blush. "Totally different! Football games are a social event. I'd go to hang out with you guys even if Sean wasn't on the team."

"Or how about girls wanting guys to change for them?" Jack said.

"Any girl who asks you to change, Jack, is doing you a huge favor," Reenzie says.

"Ha-ha," he shoots back. "Forget me, then. Superstar Sean. What do you like to do best on Sundays in the fall?"

"Watch football," Sean says immediately.

"What did you do yesterday?" Jack asks.

Yesterday was the second day of Sean and I being back together. He came over to my place in the afternoon and we watched movies . . . which I'm sure Jack already knows.

"He still watched *one* football game," I say. "He just didn't watch thirty!"

"Thirteen," Sean mutters. "There's usually thirteen on a Sunday. Three time slots. And yeah . . . I watched one. Most of one."

"Which was his *choice,*" I maintain. "I didn't make him."

I have no idea what kind of face Sean is making behind me, but I'm sure it doesn't support my argument because J.J. and Jack start laughing. I swat Sean to get him back.

"I didn't make Leo change for me," Taylor says. "I found a guy who likes the same things I like, so we can both just be totally ourselves."

I'm drinking from my water bottle when she says it and I have to force down a spit-take.

We don't come to any kind of consensus about Amalita, but I don't like what I saw. I text her that night, but she doesn't answer, probably because Denny has her watching Monday Night Football . . . which I only know is on because I caved and agreed to watch it with Sean so he could try to make me a fan. I call Ames on Tuesday and Wednesday too. I email her, I text her . . . she doesn't answer.

She thinks she can avoid me, but she doesn't know about my secret weapon. On Thursday night I write *Amalita* across my map . . .

. . . and end up in Amalita's open closet, tangled in brightly colored dresses. Since the sliding door is wide open, I see Ames posing in front of her mirror. She's wearing a clingy purple dress, a ton of jewelry, and now leans close to the glass to put a final layer of mascara on her professional-quality lacquered face.

"Aha!" I cry, jumping out of her closet.

"¡Dios mio!" she screams. She throws the mascara wand at me like it's a dagger. I scream when it hits me in the chest.

"Are you kidding me?" I wail, looking at the black scrape on my shirt. "This won't come out!"

"What are you doing here?" she asks, which I have to admit is a question I've been getting a lot lately. "How did you get in here?"

"*So* not important!" I claim, even though if I were her, I'd find it incredibly important. "Look at you! You're dressing up all alone because Denny won't let you do it when you're with him!"

"You're *loca*," she says. "I'm just trying stuff on. It's my stuff. If I want to try it on, I can. What are you, the dress-up police?"

"No," I say. "You're lying. It's Denny, and it started the minute you got together. You didn't go to Reenzie's party because he didn't want to. You stopped eating lunch with us because he likes going off campus. You stopped wearing makeup and jewelry and the clothes you like because he doesn't like you in them. You even stopped hanging out with us because he doesn't want you to!"

"He doesn't care who I hang out with!" Ames shoots back. "I'm with him and not you because I *want* to be with him!"

"Always?"

"When you were with Sean, didn't you want to be with him always?"

"I *am* with Sean," I say, "which you would know if you ever hung out with us, which you don't because Denny won't let you!"

"You don't know anything about Denny and me," she

says, and that makes me furious because I know I'm right and I can't believe she's not seeing it. If any of us acted the way she does with Denny, she'd be the first to call us on it.

"I know you never would have gotten together without me!" I say. "And you know what? I totally regret it! If I could take it back, I would!"

"Take what back? Telling Taylor and I that Kyler Leeds was in town?" Ames asks. "I was the one who saw Denny in the window that day. I got him *myself.* You had *nada* to do with it."

She's wrong again, but there's no way I can make her see it. I can't show her the map. That would be insane. I take a deep breath. "I'm not mad at you, Ames. I just think you're making a big mistake. You shouldn't have to change for this guy. You deserve someone who knows how amazing you are and likes you for that."

Whoa. Did I just kind of quote J.J.? Weird.

"He's not right for you, Ames," I continue. "Get rid of him. You'll be better off."

Ames smiles sweetly, but I feel about as safe as I felt with the evil Pomeranian I tried to save from the hot car. "Aw," she says, "you're not mad at me? You want to make me better off? That's so sweet." Then her face morphs into an evil sneer. If she had fangs, they'd be bared. "But guess what?" she roars. "I'm mad at you! You think you can sneak in here and watch me, then tell me how to run my life? *¡Vete a la infierno! ¡Vamos!*"

She points to the door.

I guess she does have a point if she thinks I snuck in here, but still. I stare at her pleadingly, hoping we can talk some more, but her face is stone.

"Amalita?" her dad's voice comes from downstairs. "Is everything okay?"

Uh-oh. I have to get out of here before he comes up and asks questions. I run into the hall, but instead of going toward the stairs and Ames's dad's approaching feet, I make sure no one can see me and use the map to write myself home.

That went nowhere near as well as I'd hoped.

13

According to Ames, I no longer exist. I know this because J.J. and Taylor both tell me so. Neither of them has seen Ames either, but they text with her and keep me posted. It's small comfort to know that Reenzie is also on Ames's Does Not Live list.

It sucks, but I try not to dwell on it. I can't force Ames to give up her boyfriend, even if he is bad for her. Besides, I need to enjoy time with my own boyfriend, because I won't see him for a week. We have a week off for Thanksgiving break, and when Aventura High's football team is knocked out of the play-offs, Sean's and Reenzie's families decide they're going to travel together to this vacation rental home in Pensacola, on the other side of the state. They leave the Sunday before Thanksgiving and won't be back until late in the night *next* Sunday—a long, Sean-free week. Taylor's gone too—she and her family are spending the week in Vermont with Taylor's grandparents. Leo's relieved. He loves being Taylor's boyfriend but says studying everything she likes and will want to talk about is so exhausting he can use the break.

Jack's going away for Thanksgiving too, and while Ames is in town, well, I'm dead to her, so that doesn't help me any. I can always pop in and see Jenna, though. We even try to bring her back to my room in Aventura one night. She's the one who comes up with the idea.

"You always bring your backpack with you. . . . Why can't you hold my hand and bring me?"

It makes sense . . . but apparently it doesn't work that way. I hold on to Jenna's left hand while I write *Home* with my right, but I pop back to my room without her.

I'm just glad it doesn't turn into a horror wreck, with me clutching her hand in Aventura, while the rest of her body's back in Maryland. That would be a tough one to explain to her parents.

J.J.'s in town for Thanksgiving break, though, and that's fantastic because my mom puts her foot down and demands I take driving lessons. Even when I finally tell her flat-out that I'm not comfortable with it because of what happened to Dad, she still says I have to.

I'm stunned, to be honest. I thought the Dad thing would be the ultimate trump card. Not that I'm using it that way—I'm genuinely terrified of getting behind the wheel of a car—but I thought for sure she'd be moved enough to let me put it off. I mean, seriously, it's only been a year. This week will be our first Thanksgiving without him. Is she not as ripped up as I am about it?

She tells me she of course is but that I need to learn to drive regardless. She has the instructor come the first Monday of vacation, and I score because I have to get my permit first, and to do that I have to first pass an online test about traffic and substance abuse laws.

The good? I stay out of the driver's seat. The bad? The test is soul-crushing, especially since I have to stare at the computer screen for around four hours and every letter jumps around like crazy. I have to bribe Erick to come in and read the stuff to me because at a certain point I just can't deal with it anymore. But I pass, and on Tuesday the instructor comes back to take me to the DMV to get my permit, then start me on my driving instruction.

I make J.J. come with me. He rides in the backseat. The instructor's up front in the passenger seat. Ten minutes into our two-hour lesson the instructor is hyperventilating, but J.J. stays calm.

"You know what, Autumn?" he says. "You're doing great. Just stay in the middle. . . . Okay, not on the median, I mean in the middle of your lane. . . . Uh-huh . . . Now flip the turn signal. . . . That's the windshield wipers, but it's good, it was getting a little dirty. . . . Okay, don't hit the blind man . . . or the children . . . or the cat . . ."

I get better. I do. It just takes a while. By the last ten minutes, the instructor even takes her hand off the phone, where she had entered 9-1 and was just waiting to see if she needed to dial that last digit. When J.J. comes with me for more instruction on Wednesday, I do even better. Honestly, at that point I feel pretty good about the world. I even take a selfie of me behind the wheel to send to Sean.

No, not while I'm actually driving.

He sends one back of his feet and the ocean, like he took it while lounging back on the sand.

He totally has the better deal for this vacation.

I miss him. As much as I gave Ames a hard time for always being with Denny—and totally stand by that—I love being with Sean. Even though we've only been back together a couple weeks, I'm used to it now. I'm used to having his arm around me when we walk, and holding his hand, and kissing him during the day, and getting together in the evenings to hang out. We text each other all the time, but it's not the same, and I've never been so excited for vacation to end and school to start up again.

I'm especially depressed Thursday. It's Thanksgiving, our first without my dad. Mom invited people over, and she told Erick and I we could too, but everyone has plans. It's just going to be the three of us plus Eddy, and we're going to eat pretty early, like fiveish, because that's already late for Eddy. Any later and she wouldn't be able to handle it.

I'm only just awake, but I hear Mom and Erick bustling around downstairs cooking. They have a whole plan to make a ton of food—way more than we need—and bring it to a homeless shelter after we take Eddy home. Mom says it's the perfect way to take our minds off our own problems and make us thankful for what we have. I get it and I'm all for it . . . I'm just too depressed to go down and help right now. I'd love to pop over and see Jenna, but I know she's doing some Turkey Trot race this morning, and the last thing I need is to show up in the middle of the course and trip her. I have a bad track record when it comes to breaking people's legs.

I hear the TV downstairs. They're watching the Macy's Thanksgiving Day Parade, just like we always did when Dad was alive. I turn it on in my room.

It makes me smile, actually. The giant Mickey Mouse float, the giant Snoopy, the big dance numbers from Broadway musicals.

That's what we should have done this year, I realize. Forget staying at home and cooking. We should have gone away somewhere exciting and amazing and different. We should have gone to New York. We should have watched the parade in person. Now we're stuck here.

A thrill runs through me as I realize something.

They're stuck here. Mom and Erick.

I have the map.

The two of them are downstairs. They think I'm still asleep. As long as I don't stay away long enough for them to miss me . . .

Keeping one eye on the TV, I pull out the map and write Macy's Thanksgiving Day Parade across it.

Next thing I know, I'm standing next to a grinning

goldfish that's twice my height. The air rings with music—
Kyler Leeds music!—and beyond it I can hear the roar of
a million voices hooting, clapping, and screaming. And
floating all around me . . . bubbles!

FUN!

I prance around, leaping up to pop bubbles as they soar
by. I realize I'm moving—I must be *on a float,* which would
explain the giant goldfish.

I laugh out loud. I'm instantly giddy—this is so cool!—
and I can't wipe the smile from my face. The cold air bites
through the long T-shirt I wore in bed, but I'm too happy
to care. As I prance around leaping for more bubbles,
I play with the other giant sea creatures in my path. I
take the hand of an enormous starfish and bow as if he
were my prince; I put my head in the mouth of a grinning
shark and flail around like it's eating me; I climb on top
of a seahorse and rear back like I'm riding him through
the ocean. Then I skip around to the other side of the
float . . .

. . . and nearly collide with a group of men and women
in fish costumes, kicking and swirling their way through
a choreographed dance. I duck to avoid flailing arms and
legs and stay low to climb to higher ground, away from
them. There's some kind of huge pink volcano-thing, and I
scale it like a mountain climber. It's tall, and the float itself
is already rolling way above the ground, so I'm pretty high
up. I peek down to see how far I've come, which is when I
realize a few things:

1. I'M ON TV! I can see the cameras! When I was playing with the fish, I was on the side away from the cameras, which is why I could just run around and play without anyone noticing.

2. I'M ON TV! What am I thinking?! Mom and Erick are watching this *right now*!

3. I'M ON TV! I really should have thought this through and changed out of my pajamas.

In addition to the cameras, I notice some security guards darting along the street toward the float. I think the fish dancers somehow reported that I wasn't part of the show. This is bad. Getting arrested will definitely put a damper on Thanksgiving. Getting arrested on live television in Manhattan . . . that's going to make for an interesting one-phone-call conversation with Mom.

Grasping for grip-holds for my hands and feet, I scurry around the pink volcano, trying to get away, but there's really no place to go. The guards are coming, and one of them has already leaped onto the float. He doesn't want to interrupt the dancing fish, so he's moving slowly, but he'll be able to grab me any second.

I need to write myself back home, but the map is in a little over-the-shoulder bag and I can't pull it out without letting go of the volcano, which would involve plummeting to the ground. "Plummeting" in general is something I want to avoid.

Not sure how I'm going to get out of this.

"Autumn?"

My name echoes all around me, and I realize that while the music of the Kyler Leeds song is still going, his voice has stopped. I look over to the side and see that I've clambered my way to the edge of the float's stage . . . on which the actual *Kyler Leeds* is standing, microphone in hand. He's dressed for the weather in a thick parka and looks stunned to see me on his volcano.

I notice the security guards have stopped moving toward me. They must think I'm with Kyler.

Okay, then.

I smile wide. "Kyler!"

I hold out a hand to him, and he helps me climb from the volcano to the stage with him. I grab his microphone. "Kyler Leeds, everyone! Put your hands together!"

The crowd loves it. They roar and start to clap. Kyler's staring at me with his mouth wide open.

"What are you—" he starts, but I don't let him finish. I put a hand to my ear, listening to the music; then when the chorus kicks in, I shout, "Sing it, Kyler!"

I give him the microphone, and I have to hand it to the guy, he's a professional. He smiles wide and sings, then slings an arm around my shoulders and holds out the microphone so I can sing with him, which I do. I even try to harmonize, but I have no clue what I'm doing. Maybe the noises I'm making will come off like on-theme dolphin squeaks.

As Kyler goes into the next verse, I look at the crowd and flap my arms up and down, rallying them to cheer more and louder. They obey. They're in the palm of my hand. I'm delirious with the power and excitement.

With a flourish, I swing both of my arms toward Kyler, and as the crowd focuses back on him, I race off the stage and climb down to the off-camera side of the float. I duck behind my old friend the giant goldfish, pull out the map, and write *Home*.

I'm standing on my bed. Someone's pounding on my door. "Autumn?" my mom calls. "Autumn?"

She rattles the knob and I thank the universe I locked it last night. Erick had threatened to make his own documentary of our first Thanksgiving in Florida, and I hadn't wanted to risk him filming me while I was asleep.

I rumple my hair and rub my eyes so they look especially bleary. I'm about to open the door when I think about my nightshirt . . . which was just featured on television. I quickly whip it off and pull on sleep-shorts and a tank, then open the door and make my voice sound half-asleep.

"I'm up, I'm up," I mumble. "Did I miss Thanksgiving?"

My mom's eyes are giant circles. Her mouth is open. She holds up a wooden spoon with batter on it, and her long curls have settled in the batter. I don't think she even realizes.

"The parade," she says. "I . . . Erick and I . . . we thought we saw you . . ."

"We *did* see you," Erick says, tromping up the stairs. "On a float with Kyler Leeds."

I look at him like he's nuts. "Loser," I say, "what are you talking about? I just woke up."

The color's coming back to Mom's face. When she speaks this time, she sounds more like herself. "It was really uncanny. He had a girl on his float who looked so much like you, I almost thought . . ." She laughs. "Maybe I'm more thrown by this Thanksgiving than I thought." She gives me a hug and tells me to come on down and help them cook. I do, but I act curious about what they saw so Erick will roll back the TiVo. It's actually not as bad as I thought. By the time I was onstage with Kyler, the TV cameras had long since moved on to the next float. What Mom and Erick saw and what freaked them out was just a quick shot of me ducking away from the fish dancers.

It was a crazy adventure, but I stand by it. I feel much better now about staying at home. I even have fun hanging out with Erick and Mom, just the three of us, and working like mad scientists to cobble together an insane amount of food. When the parade's over, we put on music—a Pandora channel we make based on one choice from each of us. We do goofy dance moves to our favorite songs, goofier ones to songs we don't like, and of course Erick pretends he's being poisoned every time a Kyler Leeds song comes on.

"I have an idea!" I say at one point. "Since Eddy's coming, I should make *boniatillo*!"

Mom and Erick freeze like I threw ice water on them.

Of course they do. *Boniatillo* is what I was making—trying to make—the day we heard about Dad's accident. It's a word I've never even said since, and it's certainly nothing I've ever wanted to try to cook. However, now . . . it just seems right.

I need them to answer me soon, though. I'm still smiling, but tears are welling in my eyes.

Then I see they're welling in Mom's eyes too. She comes over and gives me a huge hug. "I think that's a wonderful idea, Autumn. I really do."

Luckily, we have all the ingredients. Mom says she's willing to brave the supermarket for the cause, but I'd rather we all stay together. So unlike the time I made the dish a year ago, when I felt like I needed to do everything while Erick and Jenna only watched and Mom wasn't involved at all, this time we all work together. We get out sweet potatoes, sugar, lime, cinnamon, eggs, and *manzanilla*. Erick peels the potatoes, I mash them, Mom works the saucepan to stir together the other ingredients and heat it to just the right consistency . . .

We don't say anything about Dad. It's not that we don't want to; it's more like if we did, we couldn't cook—we'd just cry. But we're all thinking about him. We're all thinking about that day. And in a weird way, it's like we're doing it over again but giving it a happier ending. Maybe not one with Dad back, but one where the three of us are laughing together and having fun instead of being completely ripped to shreds.

There's still more to cook even after the *boniatillo* is done, and then we all go up to shower and get ready before we set the table. By quarter to five everything's set—Mom just has to get Eddy.

Instead she tosses me the keys.

"What?!" I say.

"You're driving," Mom tells me.

I toss the keys back to her. "Learner's permit," I say. "I can't drive alone. It's the law."

She tosses them back to me. "I'll ride in the passenger seat."

"Are you sure that's a good idea?" Erick pipes up. "They say that's the least safe place in a car. And if Autumn messes up . . ."

I should be insulted, but I actually agree. I have no desire to be orphaned on Thanksgiving . . . well, *ever*, but certainly not today, and even more certainly not when it's my fault. "Listen to your son," I tell Mom. "He has our best interests at heart."

"Erick, you're welcome to come along and sit in the backseat if you want to keep an eye on things," Mom says. "Otherwise fill the water decanter and get it on the table. We'll be back very soon."

Erick's too nervous to ride in the car with me driving, but he's also terrified to be home alone when I'm driving

Mom. He calls Mom the second she gets in the car—we can still see him through the dining room window—and stays on the phone with her the entire drive.

I actually do great. I'm pretty surprised and excited about it. The whole drive is so simple that when we turn in to the Century Acres driveway, I wheel to Mom for a high five.

"Up top for your brilliant driver daughter!"

"Autumn!"

She's looking out the windshield, so I do too . . . and slam on the brakes just in time, barely bumping the car parked in front of us.

"Oh my God!" I gasp when I realize what I did. "I'msorry-I'msorryI'msorryI'msorryI'msorry!"

Mom takes a deep breath. "It's okay. You bumped it lightly. Maybe you didn't even leave a mark. Back up a little so we can see. We'll have to talk to the car's owner and take responsibility."

I'm shaking all over—so much I can barely shift the car into reverse and back up. I do, though; then I park. I'm about to get out, when I see the driver's door of the other car open. My heart sinks. He was in the car when I bumped it. He's going to kill me.

The first thing I notice is the driver of the other car is my age, maybe just a year or two older, so I relax a little, thinking he'll understand. Then my whole body seizes because I realize the driver's not just any guy my age—it's

Kyler Leeds! He frowns as he walks toward the back of his car, but my mom's already out and talking to him.

"Hi. I'm so sorry. That was us who bumped you. My daughter's just learning and she misjudged the distance. If there's any damage, of course we'll pay for it."

She clearly has no idea who she's talking to. Kyler, meanwhile, is peering through the windshield, like he can sort of see me but wants to get a better look. Probably the sun's glare is making it hard. I get out of the car and smile sheepishly. "Hi, Kyler."

"You already know each other?" Mom asks. She still doesn't get it.

"Yeah," I say. "Mom, this is Kyler. Kyler, Mom. I mean, Gwen. Kyler's grandmother is Eddy's archenemy."

I expect some kind of amused reaction from Kyler, but he's just looking at me like my whole face broke out in a strange growth. Did it break out in a strange growth? Or is he just mad at me for bumping his car? I look down at his rear end—*the car's* rear end. "I don't see any scratches or anything," I say. "I'm really sorry."

"How did you get back here so fast?" Kyler asks. "I had a private jet waiting for me and I still barely made it."

Oh crap. I'd forgotten I spent the morning on a float with him. I feel pinpricks of sweat break out all over my body.

"What do you mean?" I ask.

"The parade. You were on my float?"

"What parade?" I ask. Then I gasp as I fake-realize what he means. "Ohhhh, the Macy's parade! I saw it on TV! Well, part of it. I slept through you. I'm sorry. But Mom says you were really good, right, Mom?"

"You're Kyler . . . Leeds?" she asks. Then she laughs and smiles. "Oh my goodness, Autumn's been a fan of yours forever. You should have seen her room back at our old house. I don't think there was a space on the walls not covered with your face. And the magazines, and the books, and the *accessories*—"

"Wow, okay, Mom, I think he gets it," I say hurriedly. But when I turn back to Kyler, he has a big grin on his face.

"What kind of accessories?" he asks.

"Not important," I say quickly.

He smiles even wider. "I'm going to get my grandmother. You sure you weren't in New York this morning?"

"On your float!" Mom exclaims. "Yes, I saw that too! The girl—she looked so much like Autumn, I thought it was her, and I knew she was up in her room."

Score one for Mom, totally coming through.

"Wow," Kyler says, "yeah. I *swore* it was you." He meets my eyes when he says it and I can tell he's still not convinced it wasn't. "Good seeing you both. Happy Thanksgiving."

"What about your bumper?" Mom asks.

"It's cool," Kyler says. "It looks fine. Even it wasn't, it's a rental and it's all covered."

Huge relief. And I got to see Kyler Leeds for the second time today! I really do have a lot to be thankful for.

We all head inside, then split off to gather our old folks. Eddy's pacing right by the door, which she tells us is what she's been doing for the last two hours. She refuses to ride in the car if "the baby" is driving—that's me—so Mom drives, Eddy takes the passenger seat, and I flop in the back. I see on my phone that Erick has texted me ten times between when we got to Century Acres and now. Apparently after I hit the other car and Mom screamed my name, she told Erick very abruptly that she had to go and hung up, and now he's in a wild panic. I call him and let him know we're okay and he doesn't have to call a SWAT team. He stays on the phone with me the whole time, and when we all get home, he runs out and hugs each one of us like we'd been at war for several years.

Thanksgiving dinner is really nice. It ends up being all about Dad, but not in an awful way. Eddy tells us stories we never knew about him as a child, and we tell her our favorite stories about him too. It's sad, but happy too. It's really the first time we've all sat around and talked about him—well, ever, really. And it's definitely the first time any of us have had a conversation like this without it getting too sad for someone to take. We do all cry a little bit, but they're tears we can talk through, and we laugh even more than we cry.

Eddy goes nuts when we bring out the *boniatillo*. She

swears it's the best she's ever had, which I find hard to believe, but I like that she says it. I know she knows its significance—we talked about it once—so I'm happy when she winks at me and takes a huge bite.

After dessert, Mom's washing dishes—I volunteered to help but she said no—and Erick and I are sitting around watching TV while Eddy's in the bathroom. It's an extended experience for her. After a while I see her in the hallway, in a spot where Erick can't see her but I can. She beckons to me and I get up and join her.

"Did you find anything in the journal?" she whispers.

"Yes," I whisper back. "It was a map. It has the *zemi* on it. It . . . takes me places."

Eddy nods. "Have you been using it to bring peace and harmony to your little corner of the world?"

I think about it. I messed up with Ames and Denny, but I was at least trying to make her happy when I got them together. And it's definitely done good things for Taylor and Leo and me and Sean. As for Jenna and I, she's straight up told me that having me at her house all the time is the best thing that's happened to her since I moved away, and it's the same for me.

"Yeah," I say. "I think I have."

"*Bueno*," she says. "Then keep doing it. "Reinaldo . . . he knows. And he's proud."

14

The next day, Mom, Erick, and I are all still floating on a cloud of family fabulousness. We wake up late, make breakfast together, take Schmidt for a walk, visit Catches Falls and play with all the dogs there, go out to the movies . . . it's all really nice, and I'm incredibly thankful for both of them.

I miss Sean, though. A lot. I'm on Day Six now (counting the day he left town, which I do), and I'm going through serious withdrawal. The texts and calls are great, but they're not enough. I need to see him, and I can't wait until Monday at school.

Do I *have* to wait until Monday?

I kind of don't.

Sean's in Pensacola. That's ten hours away by car. If I use the map and write myself there and anyone other than Sean sees me, I can say I took a road trip. Sure, it would be an illegal road trip since I only have a permit and I need an older driver in the car with me, but no one would probably think that deep about it. Plus, that's only if I get caught and need an excuse. With Sean . . . maybe I can tell him the truth. I trust him, I'm crazy about him . . . why not let him know? And once he knows, we can use the map to hang out together even more. I could even map myself into his room in the middle of the night. Not to do anything crazy, just to sleep with him. Literally *sleep* with him. Cuddle up in a bed with his arms around me and my head on his chest and tucked under the covers with him and be with him all night.

It sounds like heaven. Yeah, we'd have to scramble in the mornings to get me out of there, but even that would be easy. I'd set my phone alarm for like four in the morning and map myself to my own bed.

I love this idea. This might be the best idea I've ever had. I come up with it when Mom, Erick, and I are on our way home from the movies, and I decide I'll do it for sure this evening. Late, so Sean's not hanging out with his and Reenzie's families when I show up. It'll be dark, moonlight will stream in through the window, and I'll appear in some kind of gorgeous gauzy nightgown that flows around me like a cloud. I'll gently tap Sean awake and he'll think he's dreaming. Then I'll crawl into bed next to him and everything will be perfect.

The waiting is torture, but my plan will really only work after he's gone to bed, so it's a necessary torture. I fill the time playing board games with Mom and Erick, all of which I lose because I can't concentrate; then, after they go to bed, I put on trash TV so my brain doesn't have to even try to work. I'd love to talk to Jenna, but she's still away, and when I text her, she texts back that she's in a massive cousin conclave and can't talk, which I get. She has about a zillion cousins, and a bunch of them are our age, so when they get together it's a big party.

The whole evening, I stay in touch with Sean via text so I know when will be a good time. Obviously I don't tell him my plan, but I check in with him like everything's normal. I find out when he's having dinner, when his and Reenzie's families go for an after-dinner walk along the beach, when they all sit up playing charades, and when they finally go to bed.

That's when I start to get ready. I don't have a gauzy nightgown like the one in my fantasy, but cute sleep shorts and a tank should be good. I pull on a hoodie I like too, just in case it's cold in the house or on the beach if we want to sneak out and walk around before I make my predawn escape. I want to put on a little makeup, but I don't want it to smear while I sleep. I opt to go without it—if Ames can, so can I. I do brush out my hair with a little product and put on lip gloss—which doesn't count as makeup—and I use the body lotion Ames bought for me at the beginning of the summer that smells like coconut.

My heart is thudding in anticipation. I take one last

look at myself in the mirror to make sure the results are good; then I take out the map and write "*Sean*" across the green splotch of land.

Suddenly I'm sitting in a closet. The map seems to have a thing for closets lately. I can't see anything, but I know it's a closet because my butt is resting on a pile of clothes and shoes, many of which don't smell great.

I'm glad I have the coconut body lotion on. Hopefully its scent is stronger than the sneakers'.

Despite the odor, it's good I'm in the closet. That gives me a chance to make sure Sean is sleeping, so I can sneak up on him. There are slats on the door, but no light streaming through them. That's good. He's in bed. Or just not in the room. I adjust the slats so I can try and see.

One detail of my fantasy was right. Moonlight *does* stream into the room, so once I adjust the slats, I can see a little bit. The bed's far from the closet, but I can make out something shadowy on top of it. It's moving a little, I think. Like Sean's rolling over in his sleep.

Then I hear giggling.

Girly giggling.

My blood turns to ice.

I strain every cell to listen more closely.

I hear other sounds now. Unmistakable sounds.

Kissing.

Heavy breathing.

No-no-no-no-no-no-no. This isn't possible. I'm in the wrong room, maybe. This is one of Sean's *brothers'* rooms, and the brother's in here with his girlfriend. That has to be it.

I shift in the closet. Sneakers tumble a little under me and I freeze—did the people on the bed hear? No. They're not saying anything. I shift a little more, carefully this time, and readjust the slats so I can see the bed more clearly.

Sean and Reenzie are on the bed. They're dressed—they're both in shorts and tops—but they're smushed up next to each other and they're kissing. Not peck-on-the-cheek kissing. Not you're-like-a-sister-to-me kissing. Full-on, tongues-in-each-other's-mouths, grasping, grabbing, groping *kissing*.

I want to throw up.

I want to cry.

I want to slam out of the closet and scream at them both.

I can't. I can't do any of it. I'm not even supposed to be here. It's impossible for me to be here.

I'm so shaky I don't even know if I'll be able to write my way back home. I'm positive I'll end up in Rome, or Nome, or buried in a hole.

I get home. That's when I cry. Deep, wracking sobs that hurt when they come out.

How could Sean do this to me? How could Reenzie? Was she only pretending to be my friend all this time?

I cry until I'm completely wrung out. Then I guess I fall asleep because the sun's streaming through the window when I open my eyes. Or try to open my eyes. They're swollen and sticky and sore.

Stupid map. Peace and harmony? Yeah, right. Although I guess if I didn't see them together, I'd be living in fake peace and harmony, so maybe it did me a favor. It just doesn't feel like it right now.

I don't want to leave my room. I don't want to leave my bed. Mom comes and knocks on my door at one point to see if I want to go out with her and Erick, but I tell her I'm not feeling well. She comes and sits on my bed and pets my head—she's worried I'm not really sick, just sad after yesterday and all the talk about Dad. It would be an easy excuse, but I don't want to upset her. Plus, I liked yesterday. I don't want her to think days like that are bad. I tell her it's really just some kind of cold and I'll feel better if I just stay in bed. I don't know if she believes me, but she says okay and leaves, promising to check in while she and Erick are out.

Schmidt's the next one to come in, but him I want with me. I know he can tell I'm depressed, because he jumps on the bed, which is next to physically impossible for him, and just lies there while I hug him.

I fall asleep again, but I wake up when my cell phone rings. It's J.J.

"Hey," he says. "I was thinking about you. How did it go?"

He's pretty surprised when I burst into tears.

"I'll be right over," he says.

When I hang up, I see that Sean has already texted to say good morning. I can't deal. I change my settings and block him. By the time I do that, the doorbell's ringing. J.J. I go down and open the door, but I don't bother to fix my hair or face or get changed. I'm still in the sleep shorts and tank, my face is blotchy and swollen, and my hair sticks out in all directions, including straight up.

J.J. looks horrified for all of a nanosecond; then his face melts with sympathy and he wraps his arms around me. The hug feels really good. I hug him back and cry.

"It's okay," he says. "I'm so sorry . . . but it's okay."

Now I feel guilty. I know he thinks I'm upset about Thanksgiving without my dad. I pull away gently. "It's not what you think," I say. "Thursday was great."

He wrinkles his eyebrows. I definitely don't look like it was great.

"The day was great . . . and the dinner. It was last night." I take a deep breath and let it out in one rush along with the words, "Sean and Reenzie hooked up."

J.J. cocks his head. "How do you know?"

"I *saw* them," I say, before I realize how idiotic that sounds. "I mean . . ." I flounder to find a way I'd know it's true. "Sean admitted it," I say. "But the way he told me, I could picture it in my head, so it's like I saw it."

He still looks like he's trying to shift gears and compute what's really happening. "It's stupid," I say. "You're right—

with what you're thinking. I have bigger things to be upset about, and I'm not. I made it through Thanksgiving, and next to that, this is nothing."

"It's not nothing," J.J. says. "You can't compare it to the other thing. This is different. It's horrible. I can't believe he'd do that to you."

"You can't?" I say. "I thought you'd be giving me anagrams for 'I told you so.'"

I expect J.J. to laugh, maybe even spout out a couple anagrams, but he looks more serious than ever. "Not a chance."

There's an intensity in his eyes that surprises me. I think he's even angrier at Sean than I am. I have to admit, it feels nice that he's so protective of me and cares so much . . . but I'm not really sure what to do from here. I'm sure J.J. would be happy to hang out, but I don't think I'm up for it. "Thanks for coming over," I say.

He shakes his head. He can tell where I'm going. "Nope," he says. "Not getting rid of me that easily."

I actually laugh out loud. "I'm not?"

He shakes his head. "You've been hurt, and you need something to make you feel better. I have a car that's desperate for a road trip, and a huge list of places it needs to go, including the most amazing food spots in a two-hour radius. Get in the car."

"'Get in the car'?" I laugh. "Is that an order?"

"A firm suggestion?"

"I look like crap."

"You look beautiful."

"I'm wearing pajamas."

"Really? They look like clothes."

"I'm not hopping in your car like this."

"Come on! It'll be an adventure. You're already feeling better thinking about it, right?"

I kind of am, but I'm still not going anywhere looking like this. I compromise. I get ready, but not totally ready. I run water through my hair to tame it, then toss it in a ponytail. I slap on deodorant, put on lip gloss, grab sunglasses and flip-flops, and even though I stay in my sleep tank and shorts, I put a bandeau on underneath. I also grab my bag with my money, keys, phone, lip gloss, mints, and the map—not because I plan to use the map, but because I feel weird leaving it around the house.

"You asked for it," I say as I tromp downstairs, "the least attractive version of me you will ever see."

"Yeah, right," J.J. snorts.

"Do any of these food places have waffle cones?" I ask.

"As you wish," he replies, and opens the door for me. The humidity outside is oppressive as always, but it feels good to be out of the house. I take my usual spot in the passenger seat, slip off the flip-flops, put my feet on the dash, and turn the music up painfully loud so I can scream along.

"I hope that's helping you," J.J. says, "'cause it's killing me."

That makes me sing even louder.

J.J. wasn't kidding—he really does know a million random dives, each with amazing food. It's like a greasy-drippy-yummy culinary tour of southern Florida. We only get teeny bits at each place because we don't want to be too full for the next one. We hit up a Cuban restaurant an hour away for *pionono,* this mix of plantains and ground beef and raisins and cheese and I-can't-even-deal-with-how-good-it-is. We drive another hour for cannoli at some tiny strip-mall diner. Another forty-five minutes away there's a burger with egg and avocado and bacon on it that we have to try. . . .

It's seriously ridiculous, but it's fun. And every time we go into a new place, J.J. or I come up with new identities for ourselves, like we're undercover for the health inspector and have to ask all kinds of questions about vermin and take notes and nod inscrutably a lot. Or we're cousins of the British royal family—speaking with accents, of course—slumming on a getaway from all our lordly and lady-ly responsibilities. Or we sit really close and keep asking specific questions about the food I can eat, "for the baby."

By the time we hit our last stop, it's eleven at night. I texted Mom; she knows I'm with J.J., so she's not worried. We're at an ice-cream place that not only has waffle cones but also has *flavored* waffle cones. I can't decide which I want, so I say we'll each order a different one and share. I get chocolate chip filled with rocky road ice cream and hot fudge. J.J. gets snickerdoodle filled with butter pecan ice cream and caramel sauce. His wins. He lets me switch with him, but we're so full we can only take a few bites even though it's amazing.

The place is at the ocean, but there's no beach—just a rocky hill leading down to the water and a boardwalk that stretches over it. There aren't any rides or booths or anything on the boardwalk. It's literally just a place to walk and look out over the water, with some benches and a few lights. We walk out there when we're done eating.

"The waitress did not believe we were Cirque du Soleil," J.J. says.

"She totally did!" I shoot back.

J.J. just gives me a look.

"What?" I balk. "I could so easily pass for a Cirque du Soleil contortionist."

"You don't contort," he says.

I think about how awesome it would be if I right then and there stood on one foot and pulled the other around my neck. The problem is I can't, and if I tried I'd fall and get splinters in my face. "I can cartwheel," I say.

"*I* can cartwheel," he says.

"You cannot cartwheel."

"I absolutely cartwheel!"

"I want to see you cartwheel," I challenge him.

"Right here?" he asks. "I usually like a mat or a rubber floor . . . maybe a pommel horse."

"You do not cartwheel," I maintain.

He sighs heavily, then starts running full-speed down

the boardwalk. I can't believe it. He's really going to turn a cartwheel.

Then he stops short. "I don't cartwheel."

"I knew it! Liar!" I catch up with him and bask in my triumphant glow as we keep walking.

"You still haven't proven *you* can cartwheel," he says.

"I don't have to prove it," I say. "*I'm* not a liar."

"I only lie about things that are unimportant. The important stuff is always real."

"Important stuff like your high score in Scrabble?"

"Important stuff like how I feel about you."

He doesn't stop walking when he says it. There's no dramatic moment when he looks me in the eyes and puts his hand on my cheek. He just says it. And keeps walking. And I do too, right next to him. And I feel good all over because I know he doesn't have to make a big deal about it because it's not something earth-shattering and unexpected and will-he-or-won't-he like with Sean. It's just a fact.

J.J. loves me.

And I love him.

Not in the same way. At least, I don't *think* it's in the same way. I'm not in his head; I don't know how he feels when he looks at me. But when I look at *him* there are no fireworks. There's no flop in my stomach, or that constant electricity of space between our skin. What there is . . . is comfort. And happiness. And yeah, love. I love him. He's the best friend I've ever had. Not even Jenna would drop everything for me the way J.J. does.

So even though Sean's kind of love is exciting and life-altering . . . J.J.'s kind of love doesn't hurt. And maybe that's better.

We're so close to each other as we walk, it doesn't take much for me to reach out and twine my hand with J.J.'s. I peek out the corner of my eye. I expect him to be smiling, but he's not.

"What's wrong?" I ask.

He stops walking and turns toward me, still holding my hand. He looks at our locked fingers, then into my eyes.

"I don't want you to do something just because you're upset about Sean," he says. "That's not how I want this to be."

"I know," I say. "And it's not. What Sean did just showed me what I should have seen all along."

J.J. squeezes my hand. His pale face is even paler in the boardwalk lights. He looks small all of a sudden—like the dogs at Mom's shelter that have been abused and are worried about trying to make human friends. I've never seen him like this before, and I'm kind of amazed that it's because of me.

He laughs, but it's shaky. "I would love to believe what you're saying, Autumn, but—"

I cut him off with a kiss. He resists for a second, then wraps his arms around me and kisses me back like he's been waiting to do it forever.

15

"Blaine is out, Duckie is in!" Jenna cheers.

It's the middle of the night Saturday—or I guess super-early Sunday. I texted Jenna until she woke up so we could talk. She's still in Vermont, but she told me no one was sleeping in her cousins' basement, so I could use the map to meet her there. She described it pretty specifically so the map wouldn't mess up and land me anywhere else in the house. We were both nervous about it, but it worked perfectly.

"What was it like when he kissed you?" she asks. "Was it amazing?"

"It was good!"

Jenna winces. "Good" isn't the same as "amazing." I know it, but I'm not going to lie to her. "I mean, it's not like there were any technical problems. He's a perfectly adequate kisser."

"Ooooh, 'perfectly adequate,'" Jenna echoes. "Dreamy."

"I'm just saying, it's not like he's bad at it! He's fine. It was nice."

"Autumn, it's not supposed to be 'nice.' It's supposed to be melting into heaven. It's supposed to make you forget your name. It's supposed to take your breath away and leave you desperate for more."

"I know," I say. "That's how it was with Sean. Remember how that turned out?"

I'd already told her the whole story.

"Right, but that means Sean's a jerk, not that any guy you're crazy about is a jerk."

"Why are you giving me a hard time about this? You wanted me with Duckie."

"I did. I *do*," Jenna says, "but only if it's right. If you're not attracted to him and you only like him as a friend, that sucks for both of you."

"It's fine," I assure her. "It's great. No, he doesn't make me feel the way Sean did, but maybe he will. It just takes time."

Jenna looks dubious, but she's willing to trust me. "Did you tell Sean?"

"I texted him," I say.

"You *texted* him?" Jenna bursts.

"He *cheated* on me, remember? I did him a favor. I texted him that it's over—that's all I said. And I blocked his phone and his email. Now he can spend the rest of his vacation sliming all over Reenzie without worrying how he's going to tell me. Or *not* tell me, because I bet he wouldn't have."

"Reenzie would," Jenna says.

"Yeah, you're right," I agree. "If I didn't have the map, that's how I would have found out. Reenzie would have come into school crowing. She probably still will. Crowing and preening and hanging all over Sean . . ."

I'm getting furious just picturing it in my head, until I notice Jenna arching an eyebrow.

"What?" I ask her.

"You're pretty upset for someone with a new boyfriend," she says.

"Of course I'm upset! I told you, it'll take time for my brain to make the shift. But it will. I deserve someone like J.J. He's a million times better for me than Sean."

"Agreed," says Jenna. "If you like him as more than a friend."

It's a conversation that keeps going in circles, and I'm tired. I thank Jenna for listening, then write myself home and go to bed.

Sunday is great. J.J. and I hang out and it's just like always. I mean, honestly, is there *that* big a difference between being just friends and going out? Not really. J.J. and I have always had a great time together. Now we just hold hands a lot while we're doing it. Or he'll put his arm around me. No, I don't automatically lean against him and get all dreamy the way I did when Sean put his arm around me, but so what? It's not like I *mind* it. And kissing J.J. is nice too. I don't want to spend hours doing it the way I felt like I could with Sean, but who has hours to spend kissing? With J.J. we kiss, and then we move on and do something else more fun.

Equally fun. Whatever. It's fine. It's good. And by Sunday night Taylor and Jack are back in town and even though they both say they have whiplash from the sudden change, they're also both totally excited for us and say they always knew it would happen. That night we all watch *The Princess Bride*, which I'd never seen. Hysterically funny, but the crazy part was in the beginning, where Westley the farm boy always says "As you wish" to Buttercup. I smack J.J. on the arm. "That's what you always say to me!" I exclaim. "I thought you were all original, but it's from a movie!"

Then two minutes later, the grandpa in the movie says something like, "Buttercup was amazed to discover that when he was saying, 'As you wish,' what he meant was, 'I love you.'" Then J.J. says right along with the guy, "And even more amazing was the day she realized she truly loved him back."

He looks at me then like he couldn't possibly be any happier, and I am so blown away I kiss him right there in front of Taylor and Jack. I mean, how adorable is that? So Jack pretends to retch and Taylor gives us an "awwww," and I cuddle even closer to J.J. for the rest of the movie.

Sunday night, I'm lying in bed when my eyes snap open. It's midnight, which is exactly when Sean's getting back in town. I wonder if he'll try to call me. I wonder if he *has* tried to call me. I wouldn't know with the block on. Did he even bother, or was he relieved? Reenzie I'm sure was relieved. She probably spent the rest of the trip comforting him in his time of desperate need.

Spare me.

I make sure I look really good for school on Monday so Sean can regret what he gave up, especially when he sees me looking so good *and* with J.J. I hear J.J. pull up and beep. He's a little early, but that's probably because he hopes we'll get in some kissing before school starts. I'm cool with that, but maybe I can convince him to use the time to swing by and get a blueberry muffin from the bakery instead.

I fling open the door, ready to ask for an anagram of "morning blueberry muffin," but J.J. isn't there.

It's Sean.

Every muscle in his body is clenched, which has the beautiful effect of making each cut line in his arms and legs stand out. His blue eyes look fierce.

I want to throw myself on him and kiss him right now.

I don't, though. He blew his chance for that. I stand tall and aloof and keep my voice cool. "Hi, Sean."

"What the hell, Autumn?" he asks.

"I can't talk right now," I say. "J.J.'s picking me up and—"

"He's not," Sean says. "I called him. He said he 'agrees we need to talk.' What's going on? Why do I get a breakup *text* from you, and then I hear from Reenzie who hears from Taylor that you're going out with *J.J.*???"

Ooh. Didn't think about that part. Of course Taylor would say something to Reenzie, and of course she'd tell Sean.

So fine. He knows. Let him know. Let him understand we can both find other people who want us.

"Yeah, it's true," I say. "I broke up with you because . . ."

I'm dying to tell him what I know. Just lay it out there in detail so he can't squirm out of it. But there's no way to do it without saying stuff I just can't.

"I had a feeling," I say instead. "I felt like you were lying to me. And you want to know the truth? It hurt so bad I couldn't even deal, and J.J. was the one who helped me get through it, and *that's* why we're together now."

"A *feeling*?" Sean asks incredulously. "You got so upset from a *feeling* that you broke up with me, wouldn't *talk* to me, and started going out with someone else?"

Okay, yeah, that sounds psychotic. If it had really been just a feeling, I would have called or reached out or something. But I was totally justified in doing what I did, and he needs to know it.

"It was more than a feeling," I say. "It was like I could see it. You and Reenzie. Friday night. In your room in Pensacola." I can see it in my head as I speak, and it's like living it all over again. I'm so hurt and furious I feel myself starting to cry, but I keep talking. "You were kissing her. More than kissing her. I can't tell you how I knew but I *knew* it was happening, Sean."

Sean isn't clenched anymore. He's stunned, and a little freaked out. He even backs away from me a little.

Fine. Let him think that I'm freakishly psychic. At least it means he has to own up to it. The more he reacts, the more steely I get inside. I throw a question at him like a dart. "I'm right, aren't I?"

I expect Sean to fall apart. Cry a little maybe. Plead for my forgiveness. Admit he's a liar who's been playing Reenzie and me all along.

Instead he tenses up again. His words are clipped when he speaks.

"Reenzie told you."

"What? No, she didn't."

"Come on. You're not psychic, Autumn. Of course she told you. Yeah, it happened. Friday night, just like you said. We were hanging out with my brothers and her brothers and we got stupid and had some stuff to drink, and we went back to my room and hooked up. She spent the whole night in my room. Did she tell you that?"

I flinch away. I was wrong. I don't want to hear Sean admit any of this. I just want him to go away. But he keeps going.

"And you know what happened first thing in the morning?"

"I don't need to know what happened first thing in the morning," I say dully.

"I threw up."

"Because you drank too much."

"Because I was sick about what I did to you," he says. "Because I care about you. Because I want to be with *you*, and not Reenzie. Which is what I told her."

All the steel inside me is gone. I feel completely unhusked and so unsteady I might blow away.

"I didn't know," I say softly.

"You would've. If you'd answered my calls. Or my texts."

His eyes are so angry I don't want to look at them, but I can't look away. "I blocked you," I admit.

He grabs the lower half of his face and squeezes, then pulls down, like he has enough energy to hit something and doesn't know how to channel it. "Stupid," he says, and I don't know if he means himself or me. "I should have thought of that. The phone said the texts went through." His eyes are watery now. He's hurt, and I'd do anything to take that away.

"I was going to tell you everything, Autumn. But you didn't wait. You didn't care enough to give me a chance. You listened to Reenzie and you believed her and you went right to somebody else."

I don't think I've ever felt this horrible about something I've done. He's right—not the Reenzie part, but the important stuff . . . he's right. I should have given him a chance to explain.

I want to touch him, just to know that we still have a chance. I reach out for his hand, but he jerks away. He shakes his head. "Whatever you've got with J.J. . . . . I hope it's good. I hope it makes you happy. I'll see you around."

He turns and walks back to his car, and in that moment, when he's completely done with me, I know for a fact that *Sean's* the one I want. Not J.J. I was just too hurt to admit it to myself.

The problem is I told J.J. the opposite. I can't break up with him. It'd kill him. And even if I did break up with J.J., would Sean even want me back afterward? I doubt it.

J.J.'s car pulls up in front of the house. He gets out. He looks concerned, but happy. I want to smack the smile off his face.

That's not fair. I'm mad at myself, not J.J., but still.

"I was parked around the corner," he says. "You okay? You guys have it out?"

I nod. J.J. bends down and kisses me, but it feels like kissing cardboard. I can't let him see that, though. He'd know why. More than ever, right after seeing Sean, I need to be an amazing girlfriend to him so he doesn't suspect how I really feel. I owe him that as a friend. I kiss him back with as much feeling as I can manage, then let him hold my hand and walk me to his car.

16

Monday is a nightmare.

J.J. won't let go of my hand. If we're within touching range, he's holding my hand. If we're not within touching range, he *gets* within touching range, and then he's holding my hand. It feels like I'm locked to him. I hate it.

Reenzie's furious with me. She grabs my wrist and pulls me aside at lunch, which is the first time I see her, since I get to school so late. "Sean won't even talk to me," she says. "He's furious that I told you about what happened."

"You didn't tell me," I say. "I told him that."

Reenzie's eyes flash. "Did Taylor tell you? I'll kill her."

"Taylor didn't tell me. I just knew."

"You *just knew*?" She squeezes my wrist hard, then lets go. Her face goes from demon to Barbie doll in a split second. She even smiles. "Kind of makes sense. I mean, you know how I feel about him. You know he's interested in me. You know . . ." She gestures to her own body, up and down, because clearly no one could resist anyone who looks like her. "You figured it would happen. You're smart."

I can't tell if she's insulting me with all that, or complimenting me, or a little of both. I just keep my mouth shut and let her talk.

"I want you to know, I *am* sorry. Not that it happened. I mean, it was going to happen, but that it hurt you. I promise I wasn't thinking about you at all."

I can't even be upset with her when she says things like that. She has no clue she's being rude in any way.

"It is what it is," I say.

Reenzie grins and gives my arm a friendly squeeze. "And, hey, you're with J.J. now, which is great! I always thought the two of you would be amazing together."

She's not the only one. Taylor and Jack are still oohing and aahing over how perfect a match J.J. and I are, and J.J. eats it up. He eats his lunch one-handed so he can keep the other arm draped over me. It feels like a lead weight around my shoulders, but I don't let him know. I sit and eat and chat and smile and I don't let the smile fade even when Reenzie talks about how she's going to win Sean back, which she thinks is a fair conversation since I'm clearly with someone else.

Sean doesn't sit with us at lunch. I don't see much of him at all. He's hanging with his football friends, so maybe he's seeing Amalita and Denny. I'm certainly not. I'm still dead to Ames. Taylor's been texting with her, though, and says Amalita and her parents even had Thanksgiving with

Denny and his family at their house. I wonder if Ames wore makeup.

Sometimes I do see Sean. From a distance or across the hall. Every time I do, my heart hurts. I always try to catch his eye, and it's like throwing him my lifeline and begging him to tow me in, but he won't. He won't even look at me, even when I'm sure he knows I'm there.

The really awful thing, and the thing I feel the worst about, is that for the first time since I met him, seeing J.J. doesn't make me happy; it makes my stomach sink. I feel like I do a really good job faking it, though. It's hard, but I work at it because he deserves to feel like his girlfriend is crazy about him, and for better or worse, *I'm* his girlfriend. So I never pull away even a little when he kisses me, and I always let him hold my hand, and I try to lean in toward him when he puts his arm around me . . . all the good-girlfriendy stuff. And I try to be fun and jokey with him like we always are, and I think it goes well . . . it's just way more effort than it ever was before. I have to try, and I'm not sure how long I'll be able to fake it without him realizing.

I get the solution from Reenzie, actually. She's leaving lunch early *again* for yearbook, but when Jack gives her a hard time, she says, "You will be lucky if you *ever* see me. Yearbook is just the beginning. I'm also starting to work as an assistant for a photography professor at FSU so he'll write me a brilliant college recommendation with emphasis on my new-but-incredibly-serious passion for photojournalism. Plus, I'm starting an SAT course so when we take them in the spring, I'll be a million times readier than you."

"'Readier' isn't a word," J.J. says. "You just failed your SAT."

"And we don't have to take them in the spring," Jack said. "Fall senior year, that's what my parents said."

"That's because your parents already know you're a hopeless cause," Reenzie says.

"It's better to take them both times," Taylor agrees. "Most people do better their second time."

"Autumn did," J.J. says. He squeezes me a little closer and I'm totally grossed out because he's saying I did better going with him than with Sean, but I give a good-girlfriend giggle and sigh, "Yeah."

"Whatever," Reenzie says. "Point is, if you want to get into a good college, you have to focus your life the way we're all supposed to focus our diets to eat healthy: cut out everything except the purest forms of nutrition."

"Healthily, not healthy," J.J. corrects her. "More points off your SAT."

"I cut out everything except mac 'n' cheese, bagels, and cotton candy," Jack adds. "Is that bad?"

Reenzie rolls her eyes and leaves after that, but I'm inspired. When school ends and J.J. wants to hang out, I tell him I can't because I have an appointment with the college counselor. I don't, but his office is never very busy, so I walk right in and he's not only free to talk, but also psyched to talk. I ask him if it's true that colleges love it when you're busy following a passion and he says yes. He says grades and SATs are the most important things to them, with grades most of all. "So if you're not giving your schoolwork one hundred percent," he says, "now's the time." He says once grades are in good shape, then they look at extracurriculars like hobbies, activities, and volunteer work. Colleges want to see that you have "a singular passion, something that enriches your life so you can in turn enrich their school."

I don't need anything to enrich me, but I *do* need something to keep me busy. At that moment I decide I'll dedicate myself to getting into an incredible college. I'll devote all my spare time to studying. As for a "singular passion," I suppose I've got the whole bringing-peace-and-harmony-to-my-little-corner-of-the-world thing, but my way of doing it would be tough to explain to an admissions officer.

Of course, if I started volunteering, that *would* bring peace and harmony in a way colleges would understand, and it could take a *lot* of time. But where would I volunteer? I already help out at Catches Falls when I can, but if I spend too much time there, Mom will ask questions.

Then I realize the answer—I'll volunteer at Century Acres! It'll make Eddy feel good because I'm around. Plus, maybe I'll get to see more of Kyler Leeds. Bonus: it shows my singular passion for helping others and therefore helps me get into a great college. Double bonus: I avoid time with J.J. without hurting his feelings.

The plan is genius, and I'm pretty proud of myself for thinking of it. I practically float out of the college counselor's office, and I'm not even bothered that J.J. is waiting for me to finish. I even throw myself into his arms, kiss him, and tell him my epiphany, though of course I don't tell him why. I just say that Reenzie inspired me to take action for my life and that volunteering at Century Acres is the clear, life-changing option. J.J. even thinks it's a great idea, and he's happy to drive me there so I can check it out. He also wants to wait for me, but I tell him it might be a while since ideally I want to start volunteering right away. I tell him I'll have my mom pick me up, but I kiss him and promise to call him later.

Already I feel free. I run inside and find the manager on duty and it turns out they're totally dying for volunteers! They offer all kinds of activities—which is one of the reasons Dad wanted Century Acres for Eddy in the first place—and they need people to run them. It doesn't take experience either. They need people to start the exercise videos they play so the residents can do chair aerobics; they need people to read to the residents, to run the bingo games . . . super-easy, super-fun stuff. I tell the manager I'll start right away, but she laughs and says they're set for the day, but if I email her the times I'm free, she'll email back with a schedule.

I practically skip into the dining room to tell Eddy. She's sitting with a group of women and complaining loudly about Mrs. Rubenstein . . . who oddly enough is sitting just one table away complaining loudly about Eddy.

"Eddy!" I cry. "Guess what, *Abuela*? You'll be seeing a lot more of me, because I'm volunteering here now! I'll be here all the time!"

I expect her to stand up and announce this to the room—that her granddaughter, Autumn Falls, loves her so much she'll be spending lots of time with everyone. I figure she might even get up on the chair to dance and celebrate—it's not unlike her. Instead she pulls me close. "What happened, *querida*?" she asks softly. "Did something go wrong with the map?"

I'm stunned. I wonder if she's the one who's a little bit psychic. "No!" I say. "Why would you even think that? I just want to hang out around you and your friends. And yes, okay, it looks good on a college application."

Eddy narrows her eyes like she's sizing me up, then shrugs. "*Lo que sea*—the reason doesn't matter. It'll be nice to have you here."

She offers me a seat at the table, but I let her know I've also rededicated myself to my schoolwork and have to go study. I call Mom and she agrees to pick me up, and while I'm waiting I dial Jenna . . . but I hang up before I even finish her number. She was pretty clear that she thinks I should be with J.J. only if I'm truly attracted to him. She probably won't approve of my plan. She doesn't understand how important J.J. is to me and how much I want to make sure I don't hurt him. If I keep my schedule full enough, I can be an amazing girlfriend to him all the way through graduation. Then we can break up naturally when we go to separate colleges, and he won't get his heart broken at all.

My phone chimes. It's a text from Leo.

Need to talk! he writes. Seeing Taylor and no clue what to say!

I'd love to help him, but I don't have the energy to work on anyone else's love life. I am in fact the anti-relationship person. I am all about school and making the world a better place for the elderly.

Crazy swamped, I text back. But you've been with her awhile now. You'll do fine.

He texts back in a panic that he's positive he won't do fine at all, but I send him some smiley face emojis to help him chill out and go with it.

So now I have a whole new schedule I can ride from now through the beginning of Christmas vacation. I don't know what I'll do for Christmas vacation when J.J. wants to hang with me all the time, but I'll worry about that later. Maybe I can visit Jenna the whole time, or find a long-lost relative in someplace far away, like Los Angeles. Or China.

In the meantime, though, I'm pretty impressed with my new plan. It's productive and rewarding and the more I do it, the more I kind of think I know what it feels like to be Reenzie.

I still drive to school with J.J. every day, but I'm usually up so late the night before that we don't talk much—riding with him is like a five-minute, feet-on-the-dash power nap to get me ready for school. And no matter how much I worked the night before, I always have some more studying to do, so the minute we get to school, I give him a quick kiss, then slip into the library to crack the books. I see J.J. again at lunch, and I lean on him lovingly for the twenty minutes until I follow Reenzie's lead. When she bounces up to move on to yearbook, I bounce up to get back to the library, but I never go without kissing J.J. goodbye. After school J.J. drives me to Century Acres, and every time I thank him, he gives me an "As you wish," and I kiss him before I get out of the car.

Volunteering is actually fun. I mean, yes, a retirement home is completely high school all over again, except without the promise of getting out and moving on to something better. There are cliques, lots of stupid fights, nasty rumors . . . but I think a lot of that comes from boredom. When they have stuff to do, most of the residents just let loose and enjoy.

My time slot is after dinner, which means 5:30. I have the time between school and then to set up. The night before a shift, the manager, Liza, always emails me the activity I'll be running, so I come in ready to go. I call bingo, I deal blackjack, I put in the aerobics tapes . . . then after the first week I suggest ideas of my own, and Liza's totally up for them. Instead of *The Great Gatsby,* she lets me read them *The Hunger Games,* and they're all hooked from page one. Another day I set up a karaoke machine, and then one afternoon I convince my school's art department to donate some clay and a spinning wheel so Eddy can teach everyone how to make pots. She was a potter back in Cuba—actually a professional potter—and I can tell it makes her feel alive to be back behind a wheel. I promise myself I'll save up some allowance so I can buy her a pottery wheel of her own.

Anyway, including my cleanup time, I'm at the Acres— yeah, that's what those of us who are "in" call it—until around seven, at which point I call Mom and she picks me up and I dive hard-core into homework . . . which honestly takes me until midnight; then I go to sleep and start all over again the next day. Weekends I give a couple hours to Catches Falls and a couple hours to the Acres, and the rest of the time I need to finish up all the work I can't get to during the week.

It's a tough schedule! But it's great for a million rea- sons. Yes, the J.J. thing, of course, but the truth is I've never been better than a B, B– student. After only the first week, every single one of my teachers came up to me to say they've noticed my hard work, they're excited about it, and they think if I keep it up, I can get my grades up to As. When I tell that to Reenzie at lunch about a week into my new schedule, I think she's even more excited for me than my mom is.

"And that makes two of us with exciting news," she says coyly. Then she leans in closer to the group. "Sean and I are going out."

The entire world stops. I'm leaning against J.J., and I

can feel his body stiffen around me, wondering how I'll react. Jack's looking at me like he's inspecting me. Only Taylor's attention is on Reenzie.

"That's so fantastic!" Taylor squeals.

"Totally not a surprise," I say, and I even surprise myself with how calm I sound. "I mean, the two of you . . ."

"You called it, Autumn," Reenzie says. "You knew even before I did, remember?"

She's talking about my "feeling" that she and Sean were together in Pensacola. I feel my fists clenching and pulling up grass, but I force them to relax. I smile even wider.

"Yeah, well, you know," I say, "I guess now we're both with the right guys for us."

Does my voice sound as stretched and tinny to everyone else as it does inside my head? I hope not. Just to make sure, I turn my head and give J.J. a kiss. When I turn back around, Jack's eyes have narrowed. What is up with him?

After that day, Sean goes back to having lunch with us. He seems to have no problem making eye contact with me now that he's completely entangled with Reenzie. And when he does look at me . . . there's nothing there. No longing, no anger, just . . . blandness. I'm just another person to him.

After that I stop joining everyone for lunch. I hate to do it so quickly after the Sean-and-Reenzie news because I don't want it to be obvious that's why I can't hang, but I just can't. The good thing is that the semester is about to end and finals are coming up, so I have very good reasons to spend lunch in the library with a Quest Bar.

Additional Perk: less J.J. cuddle time. And less time with Jack, who I swear is starting to give me the evil eye whenever I see him. It's the same way he looks at Carrie Amernick sometimes, and I wonder if Jack is actually obsessed with Carrie because he wants to date her or because he's upset that when she and J.J. were together, she was taking away J.J's friend time. If that's the case, he shouldn't be upset with me at all. I'm giving J.J. plenty of friend time.

Honestly, I'm feeling so good about things I wonder if I couldn't use this experience as a slam-dunk college essay. "How I Protected My Best Friend's Feelings, Brought Joy to the Elderly, and Skyrocketed My College Transcript, All While Saving Myself from a Broken Heart." I think it's brilliant. I'm even composing it in my head one night while I'm leaving Century Acres.

I'm in my third week volunteering. There are just a few days left until Christmas break—which I still haven't figured out how I'll handle, but I'm confident I'll come up with a fabulous plan—and I'm heading out after a particularly awesome social media tutorial session. I helped a bunch of the residents use the computer room—which is amazing but nearly always empty—to set up Facebook, Twitter, and Pinterest accounts. Most of them are a little freaked out by the technology, but when I show them how they can use the accounts to follow—and therefore spy on—their kids and grandkids, they're totally psyched. Unfortunately, Eddy takes the class, so now I'll have to watch what I pin and tweet.

I'm walking out the door and am about to call my mom for a pickup when I nearly slam into Taylor.

I'm surprised to see her. The play goes up in just a couple days, and they're in dress rehearsals every night. She still has her hair pinned up like Sarah Brown, and she's wearing all her stage makeup.

She looks furious. I can't imagine what she's doing here. As far as I know, she'd only be here to see me, but why?

"Hey!" I say. "Are you okay? Did something go wrong at rehearsal?"

"*Very* wrong," she says. "Leo broke up with me."

Unbelievable. He was crazy about Taylor—he couldn't keep their relationship up *at all* without my help?

"Wow," I say. "I'm really sorry."

"You want to know *why* he broke up with me?" Her face twists with even more fury, and I get a bad feeling I know exactly why.

Leo had told her everything. How I fed him things to say so they'd seem right for each other. He'd even shown her my texts, which he swore he'd delete. He'd told her he was totally crazy about her and really wanted to be her boyfriend, but it was too hard turning himself inside out to be the kind of guy she'd like. He'd wanted to stay together, but only if he could just be himself.

"And you know what I told him?" she asked. Her face burned bright red even through the stage makeup.

"No?" I asked.

"No!" she wailed. "I said yes! That's how much I like

him! So we went for a walk outside the theater to talk . . . and said *nothing* for a half hour!"

"Wow," I said. "Nothing?"

"Nothing that went anywhere. 'So how did you like today's run-through?' I asked. 'I'm actually kind of *sick* of talking about the show,' he said. 'Okay,' I said, 'Well I looked into some more theater schools. Can I talk to you about them?' 'Actually,' he said, 'I think it's really dumb to go to theater school because it totally limits your options'!"

"Ooooh." I wince. "I told him not to tell you that."

"What is wrong with you?!" she yelled. "Why did you Cyrano me?"

I have no idea what she's saying. "Why did I . . . what?"

"Faked it. Why did you have Leo fake a relationship with me?"

"It wasn't fake!" I say. "I mean, not totally. He really liked you. He just didn't know you."

"Which means he didn't like me!" she shoots back. Her coiffed hair is starting to fall out of its bobby pins as she leans over me and roars, "He just thought I was pretty!"

"Well," I say meekly, "you *are* pretty."

"Autumn!"

I give up. I have to tell her. "It's just because you were pining over Ryan and I hated to see you wasting your time with him when you could be with someone who really liked you—"

"Wasting my time with him?" she snaps. "Because he's gay?"

"So you found out," I say. "He *is* gay!"

"*No!*" she retorts. "He's *not*. He's very straight, and I found out in the dressing room today that he was totally interested in me, until I started going out with Leo."

All of a sudden, I feel very small.

"Oh," I say. "So, um . . . maybe you could go after him now?"

"Now he's with the girl playing Miss Adelaide," she says, folding her arms over her chest. "Thanks to you. And your help. And the fake boyfriend you gave me in my real one's place."

I've never seen Taylor this furious. Not even when she was fighting with Amalita.

"I'm sorry," I say.

She purses her lips together. "Yeah," she says coldly. "You really are." She turns on her heel and stalks toward her car, but turns around to add, "Do me a favor and don't come to the show. I'll do a lot better if I don't have to see your face."

Now she really does spin and walk away, and I'm so shocked I'm frozen in place. Literally can't even move.

Taylor just dumped me.

I'm still staring at the spot where her car pulled away when someone snaps their fingers in my face.

"Yo. Autumn," a guy says. "If you're trying to get the old folks to play freeze tag, you'll be standing here a long time."

I blink and look at the guy. "Kyler!"

17

Kyler Leeds puts his fingers to his lips. "Keeping it on the down-low, remember? Everyone's been really good about it. No need to shout it to the world."

"Like you're the only Kyler in the world?"

"Know a lot of others?"

I have to admit I don't. I change the subject. "What are you doing here?"

"What do you think I'm doing here?"

"Isn't Meemaw asleep? Eddy goes to bed the minute my activities are over."

"No." Kyler laughs. "Meemaw likes to stay up and watch the *Tonight Show* and *Late Night*. She'll be up for a while. Speaking of up"—he gazes at the top of the building—"you ever been on the roof of this place?"

"There is no roof access," I say. "They don't want the residents having any accidents. Not those kinds of accidents," I add, at Kyler's raised eyebrow.

"There's no roof access for you regular people," Kyler says. "But if you happen to be an international rock superstar with a grandmother who likes little adventures . . ."

He takes out his wallet and pulls out a magnetic key card. He waggles it in front of my face.

"Are you sure you're an 'international rock superstar'?" I ask "'Cause I usually hear more like 'pop icon fad.'"

Kyler winces and puts a hand over his heart. "Ow. And this from a girl who wallpapered her room with my face."

"It's sad, with my mom," I say. "The senility. She doesn't always know what she's saying."

He flashes the key card in my face again. "Come on. You'll like it."

We walk inside and he and the guy at the front desk exchange a secret, knowing nod. To me the guy says, "Excuse me, ma'am, do you have an ID?"

"It's me, Autumn," I say. "I was just in here ten minutes ago."

"ID?"

"I see you every day," I maintain. "You never ask for ID."

The guy looks nervously at Kyler, then says, "That can't be true. Here at Century Acres, we provide the top security for our residents, including checking the IDs of every visitor who enters."

"Better show him your ID," Kyler says, amused.

I dig out my Aventura High ID and show it to the guy, then follow Kyler inside.

"Think he'd work that hard to impress a pop icon fad?" Kyler asks as we walk. "I don't think so."

We go to the elevator and he waves his key card at a panel I never paid attention to before, then presses a button with no number next to it, which I also never noticed before. Eddy lives on the first floor, and all the activities are on the first floor too. I don't think I've ever even been in this elevator.

When it stops, we step into the hot, muggy night.

"I grew up in Philadelphia," Kyler says. "I still can't believe this is what it feels like here this close to Christmas."

"I know," I say. "I grew up in Maryland. It's freezing there now."

The roof itself is nothing special, just a huge flat sprawl. But Kyler leads me to a simple lounge setup. There are a couple chaise lounges, a large chest—like a toy chest— small drink tables, folding chairs, and . . .

"Is that the comfy chair from downstairs?" I ask.

"One just like it," Kyler says. "The other stuff was up here before. The staff come up here to chill out on breaks. I had the chair made just for Meemaw. If you tell your grandmother about it, I'll have to kill you."

He opens up the toy chest, which is actually a blanket chest, and takes out a thick fuzzy throw rug. He lays it out and lies on it, then pats it so I'll lie next to him. "Trust me," he says. "You'll like it."

And suddenly my heart remembers that this is *Kyler Leeds,* and I'm all alone with him at night, on a roof lit only

by the moon, stars, and a couple safety lights near the elevator. I've been cool up until now, but I feel myself get
quivery. Still, I sit down on the rug next to him.

"Now lie back," he says.

I do.

With the high wall around the edge of the roof, there's
not much of a view when you stand up. Lying down it's a
whole different story. An eternity of stars dot the sky.

"There's the Big Dipper," Kyler says.

"Where?"

He rolls onto his side, moving closer to me, and takes
my hand. I tingle all over as he points it up at the sky, tracing the outline of the constellation.

"And there," he says, moving my hand to another spot,
"is the Little Dipper."

I have no idea if he's tracing any real constellation at
all. I just like that he's touching me. It's hard to keep my
breath steady when he's this close.

"Any others?" I ask.

"Oh sure," he says huskily. "But if you really want to see
stars . . ."

He reaches over to my far shoulder and gently turns my
body so it's facing his. We're both lying on our sides now,
staring at each other barely an inch away, all alone on a
cozy rug. He's my whole field of vision now. Everything I see
is Kyler Leeds. His dirty-blond hair, his light freckles, his
green eyes, his perfect teeth, the tiny mole on his left cheek-
bone. I've had his whole face memorized for years. I used to

kiss his poster before I went to bed at night. I've dreamed of a moment just like this, and now it's actually here.

"Hi," he says.

The single syllable sizzles all over me. I'm not sure I can even find my voice to say anything back.

"Hi."

He leans closer, and while part of me is right there in the moment experiencing it, another part has leaped out of my body and is jumping up and down, shouting to the universe, "KYLER LEEDS IS ABOUT TO KISS ME!!!!"

Our lips touch, and every star in the sky explodes in my head.

But I pull away.

"What's wrong?" he asks softly.

"Nothing," I say. "Seriously, *nothing's* wrong. But I can't. I have a boyfriend."

"It's okay," he says. "I have girlfriends."

He leans in for another kiss, but I can't help it. I start to laugh. "Girl*friends*? Like, more than one?"

That breaks the spell. I sit up. Kyler doesn't spend that much energy. He just props up on an elbow.

"Well, yeah," he admits. "Is that a problem?"

"Of course it's a problem! Is that not usually a problem?"

He raises an eyebrow. Of course it's not usually a problem. He's Kyler Leeds. Most girls would kill to be on his list of girlfriends. I roll my eyes. "For me it's a problem. My life is complicated enough without kissing some guy I have to share with a bunch of other girls."

"I like complicated," Kyler says.

"I'm still not kissing you," I retort.

"That's okay, lay it on me. What's so complicated?"

"You really want to know?"

"Yeah," he says, and I kind of think he's serious, not just playing along to try and get me to kiss him again. Even if I'm wrong, I'm dying to talk it all out with someone, so I tell him. Everything. I fudge the truth a little about the map, but I tell him about Ames and Denny; Taylor and Leo; and every bit of drama between myself, Sean, Reenzie, and J.J.

"So I did all these things because I wanted to make things better, but I made them worse. And now Taylor and Ames hate me; Sean doesn't care about me because he has Reenzie and he thinks I love J.J.; and even though J.J.'s my best friend in the world, I can't handle being around him because it's so hard to pretend I like him that way when I don't . . . but if I tell him the truth, I'll crush him and we'll never be friends again. And Jack . . . I don't know what's up with Jack. He's just insane."

"He's standing up for his bro," Kyler says.

"Standing up how?" I ask. "I'm his bro's girlfriend. He should be nice to me."

"Except you're not being nice to the bro."

"I am so being nice to him! Weren't you listening? I'm bending over backward to be an amazing girlfriend to him! He has no idea I'm not totally into him."

"I bet he has an idea," Kyler says. "You're not as smooth as you think."

"I am incredibly smooth."

"You're not, and I can prove it. I don't believe for a second that it wasn't you on my float at the Macy's parade."

My jaw drops. I'm still searching for an answer when he continues.

"No big deal. You don't have to tell me how or why, but I know it was you, and your smooth denial was a joke. So here's what you have to do: talk to all your friends. Be honest. Totally honest. Tell them what you did and why you did it. Tell them how you really feel. Tell them you're sorry. Just be real."

I laugh out loud. "Easy for you to say. You're Kyler Leeds. If you want to apologize to someone, you just sing about it and they forget they were ever upset."

"Or they sue me," Kyler says. "That's happened too. But, yeah, most of the time the song thing's a pretty cool way to go." Then he gets to his feet. "I should go down and see Meemaw. Unless you've changed your mind about the kissing thing?"

"Tempting," I admit, "but no."

He shrugs; then we both get off the blanket. I call my mom while he puts it away, and we ride down in the elevator together. He kisses my cheek before he gets off on the second floor. "See you around, Autumn."

Maybe it's good I'm not speaking with Taylor and Ames. If I were, it would be torture keeping this night from them. I replay the kiss in my head as I wait for Mom and all the way home. When we get there, a familiar car is parked in front of the house, and all the joy fades out of my evening.

It's J.J.

I tell Mom I'll be in soon, then take a second to arrange my face. I need to look happy to see him. Smiling, I dart out of the car and walk-run to J.J.'s, like I'm so excited to see him I can't help but bounce a little. He sees me coming and gets out of the car, then walks around to lean on the passenger side. That's where I bounce up to him.

"Hey, you!" I chirp. I throw my arms around his neck and kiss him.

He doesn't put his arms around me or kiss me back. He keeps his hands in his pockets. I pull away a little and see he looks sick. Illuminated by the streetlights, his cheeks are drawn. His hair hangs limply in his face. His body is tense, but hunched somehow. Defeated.

"What's wrong?" I ask.

He meets my eyes. His are sad and watery.

All of a sudden I'm scared.

"J.J.?"

I reach for his hand, and for the first time in weeks, I mean it. I want to touch and comfort him. I want to help. But he won't move his hands out of his pockets.

"I'm breaking up with you," he says.

Part of me is suddenly energized. This is perfect. *He's* breaking up with *me*! I get what I want, but it's not my fault. I'm not breaking his heart. He's doing what he wants.

But if that's true, why does he look so sad?

"Why?" I ask.

"Because that's what you want," he says, "but you don't have the guts to do it yourself."

"J.J., that's not true!"

I can't help saying it. I want to make him feel better. But he grimaces like he smells something rotten.

"Stop! Just stop lying to me! I *told* you—from the very beginning, I told you—please don't do this if it's just about Sean. I said that."

"I know, but—"

"But you didn't care, because you weren't thinking about me. You were thinking about you and what felt good for you when you were sad."

"No! I was thinking about you and how much I care about you—"

"Care about me," J.J. echoes. "Autumn, I love you. I'm totally, head over heels in love with you."

The words hurt. They shouldn't, but they do. Then his eyes fill with tears and it's so painful I can't even take it.

"You didn't have to kiss me," he says. "You had what you wanted from me. I was happy to give it. Why did you kiss me? Why?"

His eyes beg for an answer. I don't have a good one.

"I don't know," I admit.

"Me neither," he says. "But I really wish you hadn't." He looks down at the ground. "I can't drive you to school anymore," he says, "or to your grandmother's. I can't be your farm boy. Honestly . . . I'd rather just not see you for a while."

"What? J.J., come on. That's crazy. You're my best friend."

"Maybe," he says. "But you're not mine. I've got to go."

There's a catch in his voice, but he races around to the driver's seat, gets in, and zips away before I can see him cry.

18

So that's it. I officially have no friends. Except for my group at Century Acres. They love me.

On the plus side, I think I ace my finals, and the college counselor is very impressed with the way I've "turned over a new leaf." He's especially encouraging since PSAT scores came back and I didn't do very well. But since I took them when I was Old Autumn, he's confident they won't reflect the SATs New Autumn will take in the spring.

On the minus side, I spend the last few days of school before Christmas break completely alone, floating through the halls like I'm invisible. It's almost worse than last year, when I was scorned and hated but at least known. Now I'm a phantom.

I keep my schedule. I just walk to school, and I take the bus to Century Acres after or have Mom drive me if I have supplies to carry. And I've decided I'll start driving lessons again, so in a few months I'll be able to get places on my own.

I'm convinced Christmas break will be long and misera-ble, but Mom surprises Erick and me with a trip to Disney World and Universal. Between the two parks, we're there for ten days—we're even there for Christmas. When Erick and I first hear about it, we're upset because it's not the kind of Christmas we used to have, but Mom says that's the point. She wants to try new things and find new tradi-tions.

The trip is perfect. We stay at the Pop Century Resort in Disney, which is goofy and cheesy and fun, and we go through all the parks and pose with characters, and in the evenings they make it fake-snow on Cinderella's castle, and we go to the water parks even though it's December and it's surreal, and at Universal we ride wild roller coast-ers and pretend we have Harry Potter magical powers . . . and for those ten days I forget everything. I don't even bring the map with me; I lock it up in my room. It's waiting for me when we get back, along with every other depress-ing thing in my life. I pick it up and take it to my bed. I stare at the *zemi* on the back.

"I know you show up to help me," I say. "I know you're all about me bringing peace and harmony to my little cor-ner of the world. But every time I use you, I mess up my life. Why? What am I doing wrong?"

The *zemi* doesn't answer, but at least it doesn't disap-pear like the one on the journal did. I decide to tuck it away. I've caused enough trouble. Better to leave it be for a while.

It's only four days before New Year's when we get back from the trip, but it's the day of Century Acres' holiday party. It's not a coincidence—they never hold the party on Christmas Day because a lot of the residents go see their families, and the manager wanted to wait until I could be there, "since you've made such a profound difference in their lives."

That feels good to hear. I'm not a total screwup, I guess. Just with people under the age of eighty.

By the time Mom, Erick, and I get to the Acres, the party is in full swing. The lobby's decorated, there's a huge Christmas tree, and a Hanukkah menorah, and a Kwanzaa kinara. There's a manger scene, but someone moved all the sheep into compromising positions, which Erick thinks is hysterical. I secretly do too, but I feel like as a volunteer I should be more proper about this kind of thing, so I break up the lovefest and put them back in place.

Lots of residents are thrilled to see me, which feels pretty terrific. They tell me how much they missed me and how much more fun it is when I run the activities here, and Mom and even Erick are impressed because they didn't really know what I was up to all those hours here.

Then I see a true Christmas miracle.

Eddy and Mrs. Rubenstein . . . *dancing* together. They're doing some kind of swing move to the music pumping through the speakers and they're making a mess of it, but they're laughing together like old friends.

"Wow!" I say as I walk over to them. "Are you guys actually okay with each other now?"

"Your Eddy is a doll," Mrs. Rubenstein says, and Eddy adds, "Zelda is *la buena gente*. And her grandson's music isn't so bad."

"She came over to play cribbage yesterday and I played her all his albums," Mrs. Rubenstein says.

"I like the one with the panting and the moaning," Eddy says.

"All right, then," I say. "I'm just going to check on the cookie situation."

"Wait, wait," Mrs. Rubenstein says. She grabs her purse from a chair and rummages in it. She pulls out an envelope and hands it to me. "Here. He left town for a tour, but he wanted me to give this to you. Merry Christmas."

I open the envelope. There's a flash drive inside.

I can't wait until after the party to look at it on my computer. I need to know what's on it *now*. I duck away from the party and go to the computer room. It's empty, so I have my choice of machines. I plug the drive into one and fire it up.

Six files on the drive.

Amalita

Taylor

Sean

Reenzie

Jack

J.J.

I click on the Amalita file first. It's a video.

"Ames! Hey, it's Kyler Leeds. We met last spring at the Night of Dreams, remember? Look, I've been talking to Autumn, and she feels awful about how she handled the Denny thing. She really wants to talk to you, and you'll be doing me, Kyler Leeds, a huge personal favor if you get yourself to Autumn's house for a party on New Year's Eve. And remember, there's nothing like a new year for second chances."

Whoa.

I click on the others, one by one. The Taylor, Sean, Reenzie, and Jack files are similar to Amalita's. They start with a hello from Kyler, some personal touch to prove he actually knows their stories (like for Jack's he says, "So, Jack, I know you think I'm pretty much a tool . . ."), and then he says what I feel awful about and that they should come to my New Year's Eve party and that the new year is a time for second chances.

J.J.'s file is a little different. This time Kyler's holding a guitar.

"My man J.J.," Kyler says. "I hear you think I'm gay, so I hope you don't think I'm coming on to you, 'cause I'm not. Though from the way Autumn talks about you, if I were gay, maybe I would. You sound pretty cool. But here's the deal. Autumn is all kinds of ripped up about what's going on with you two, but she's having a nasty time figuring out how to say it without killing the really special thing you guys have. As far as I know, there's only one good way to get out the really deep, complicated stuff, and since Autumn's too tone-deaf to do it on her own . . ."

He starts playing the guitar and singing. It's a song called "As You Wish"—or at least, I think that's what it's called because that's what kicks off the chorus. It's not one of Kyler's regular songs. It's new, written specifically about J.J. and me, and has a million little details that I didn't even realize Kyler heard when I told him the story. It sums up everything—how much I really do love J.J. Maybe not the way I wish I did, and maybe not the way he loves me, but in a way that's real and deep and means more to me than any random boyfriend possibly could.

I get teary when I hear the song, and I wonder if J.J. will too.

When it's over, Kyler looks right into the camera. "Come to Autumn's house New Year's Eve. She's having a party, but it won't be a party without you. It's a brand-new year, J.J.—the perfect time for second chances."

I'm blown away. I can't believe Kyler did this for me. I don't know what's more shocking: that he took the time to write the song and make all these videos or that he paid close enough attention to my rambling to know what to say in them.

I guess I was right to be obsessed with Kyler Leeds for so long. He's a pretty impressive guy.

I sign on to my email and send the files to my friends right away.

I haven't even ejected the flash drive before my phone rings. It's Ames. I haven't even heard her voice since our big fight.

"Are you kidding me?" she wails. "*¡Estas jugando!* That's *Kyler Leeds!*"

"Yeah," I say.

"How do you know Kyler Leeds?" she screams.

"Ames, I love you, but you're kind of hurting my ear."

"I'll hurt your face if you don't explain how you know this boy," she retorts. "And I love you too. And not just because you know Kyler Leeds, but *you know Kyler Leeds*!!!!"

"So you'll come to the New Year's party?"

"*¡Sí, sí!* But not to make up. I'm making up with you right now. You were right. Denny was *muy loco*. But he was hot and he was a senior and he was a football god and oh, Autumn, the stuff he told me—that I was *soooo* beautiful and *soooo* wonderful and *soooo perfecto* . . . as long as I didn't do this and this and this and this and this."

"You broke up with him?"

"While you were away. I wanted to call you, but *soy terca*— too stubborn to do it. But then you sent me *Kyler Leeds*!!!!"

"He won't be at the party."

"He won't?"

"Still coming?"

220

"Don't be *estúpido*! Of course I'm coming! I'll stay the night before and help you set up. But we need to talk before that because, Autumn, our boy J.J. . . . *dios mio,* you've done that boy wrong."

I wince. "I know. Believe me. I'm trying to make it up to him."

My phone beeps. I look at the screen.

"It's Taylor," I say.

"Conference her in!" Ames cheers.

I do, and Taylor immediately screams, which makes Amalita scream; then the two of them scream together. At least if my eardrums get blown out on this call, I'm in the right place to borrow hearing aids.

"Yes-yes-yes-yes-yes!" Taylor cries. "I will come to the party and I forgive you, as long as you promise to stay out of my love life from now on."

"I promise," I say.

"Unless you want to fix me up with Kyler Leeds," she notes. "Then that's perfectly acceptable."

"Was your video the same as mine?" Ames asks.

"I don't think so," Taylor says. "Mine congratulated me on *Guys and Dolls*. He said he knew from our karaoke night that I'd be great in musicals. I wish he could have seen it." She gasps. "There's a DVD of the show! Autumn, do you think you could get it to him?"

"I can try," I say. "I can't promise he'll watch it."

"Oh!" Ames gasps. "You should get him to perform at our junior prom!"

"Yes!" Taylor agrees.

"Guys, I can't do that," I say. "I would never ask him for something like that. I didn't even ask him for the videos. He just did them."

Now they want to know the millions of details about how my life entwined with the life of the greatest celebrity in the universe, and I tell them the most believable story I can think of that doesn't reveal anything about him hanging at Century Acres. I say he was impressed that I gave my friends the Night of Dreams with Kyler Leeds, he emailed to tell me so, and we started writing back and forth. They of course want to see all his emails, but I say he asked me to delete them so they couldn't possibly leak to the press, and I did as he asked. Normally I think both Ames and Taylor would yell at me for that, but since they have their videos, they're cool.

The three of us talk forever, and it feels so good to have them back that I totally forget about the holiday party in the lobby until Mom pokes her head into the computer room.

"Autumn," she says, "Erick and I have been looking for you everywhere. The party's over. We need to go home."

I apologize, then hang up with Taylor and Ames, both of whom want to come over tomorrow so we can keep talking.

"Um, Mom?" I ask in the car on the way home. "Do you mind if I have a New Year's party?"

19

Mom actually loves the idea of a New Year's Eve party, but she doesn't want it to be just mine. She invites Amanda and a bunch of her other friends from Catches Falls and the yoga studio she goes to, and Erick invites Aaron and several of his other friends. Even Schmidt's having a friend come. Our neighbors Kevin and Pete have a dog named Sugar, who has fallen completely in love with Schmidt and follows him around on all his walks. When Mom invited the guys, she invited Sugar too. So even if my love life is still in shambles, Schmidt at least will have someone to kiss at midnight.

The day after I send out the Kyler Leeds messages, I get a call from Reenzie.

"Is this real?" she asks.

"The party," I say, "or Kyler?"

"Both," she says.

"Both real," I tell her.

She doesn't say anything for a little while, and I wonder if she's thinking of the Night of Dreams last spring and how she was supposed to meet Kyler but didn't. I kind of expect her to be mad when she speaks next, but she's not.

"Sean won't show me his video," she says. "Are you going to try and get him back?"

Whoa. Reenzie doesn't sound mad; she sounds *scared*. Of me. Stealing her boyfriend. Like Autumn Falls could ever steal Reenzie Tresca's boyfriend. Not that I'm over Sean—I'm actually still completely in love with him, and maybe if they break up one day I'll have a chance with him again—but I'm not thinking about that now.

"I would never do that," I promise her. "You're together. He's not available."

"You're sure?"

"Not until you get married to college-guy. Then Sean and I have a wedding fling, right?"

"An epic wedding fling, Autumn. One we'll all be talking about for ages."

Then she tells me both she and Sean will be at the party. As for Jack, he texts me later that day. *Okay, because he admitted he's a tool, I'm there.* Then he sends me a Vine of Kyler's video to him, edited down to Kyler saying, "I'm a tool" over and over again.

I don't hear from J.J. at all. Ames tells me he's still not sure if he's coming.

"Did he listen to the song?" I ask.

"Won't tell me," Ames says. "I don't know."

I'm sad, but I get it. And in the meantime, we all throw ourselves into party planning. It's totally last-minute, but Mom wants to do it up big-time. She hires a caterer, and Taylor and Ames practically move in to help us decorate and make music playlists and get the house perfect. By the thirty-first, it's a whirlwind of black, silver, and gold, with streamers, balloons, banners, colored lights, a disco ball . . . it kind of reminds me of our old Halloween parties, except with a different theme. A theme of second chances, like Kyler said. Or starting over.

Guests start arriving around seven. Mom, Erick, and I decided to each dress in one of our theme colors. I'm in a sleeveless silver shimmery dress, Mom went with a little black dress, and Erick sports a seriously impressive gold tux. He sets up his camera on a tripod so we can pose in front of it and make a little video. Mom starts by announcing the date—so when we have a whole stack of these, we'll know which year is which.

By eight o'clock, our house is completely full. We're blasting music inside and out, people are dancing, Eddy and Mrs. Rubenstein are chatting together on the couch, and everyone seems really happy. I've been so busy running around and taking people's wraps and bags that I haven't had the chance to enjoy the party yet, but now I mingle. Taylor and Ames look like Christmas. Taylor's in a green cocktail dress, while Amalita's wearing a red sheath that clings to her gorgeously. She's made up to perfection, and she jangles when she walks from all her jewelry. They both look spectacular. They pull me outside to our make-shift dance floor. Jack's already there, trying to impress Amanda's fourteen-year-old daughter with his moves. I think they look ridiculous, but she's laughing, so maybe he's doing okay.

I excuse myself when I see Sean getting sodas at the drinks table. He's wearing jeans and a dark blazer, with a white shirt that stands out against his dark skin. I have to catch my breath before I get too close, or I can't trust what I'll do.

I sidle up next to him.

"Hey," I say.

"Autumn, hi," he says.

I can feel the space between us sizzling, like it always has. Everything in me wants to seal that space and curl into his arms, but I can't. He's with someone else. He probably doesn't even think of me that way anymore.

Here it is, our first real conversation since he came to my house after his trip, and I have no idea what to say.

I notice him glance behind me. I turn around and see Reenzie. She's inside, but she's looking out through the sliding glass doors. She smiles and waves like everything's okay, but even from this far away I see she's a little worried. I figure I have about a minute with Sean before she comes out and links herself onto his arm.

"I saw the video," Sean starts.

Kyler had said on it that I did what I did because I was angry and hurt, but I should have given him a chance to explain and I was sorry. He also said my feelings hadn't changed.

"It's stuff I should have told you myself," I say.

"Maybe," Sean says. "Maybe if you had . . ."

He sighs, like he's not really happy with the way things turned out, and I surprise myself by getting a little mad. He's with Reenzie. If he's not totally happy with her, he shouldn't be with her. It's just as bad as what I was doing with J.J.

"That's the real problem!" I say it like I'm making a discovery, because I really am. "You can't make up your mind. Even before you kissed Reenzie, you were texting us both all summer, sending us the same pictures, flirting with us. . . . I totally thought you were interested in just me, and Reenzie was just as positive it was her."

Sean looks uncomfortable. "I *do* like you both. In totally different ways."

"But that's not okay! I mean, I guess it's okay if you like us both, but you have to make a real choice. You know the real reason I went out with J.J.?"

"You were mad at me," Sean says.

"No. I went out with him because he told me I deserved someone who didn't flop around. Someone who was *positive* he wanted to be with me."

"I *was* positive."

"You weren't! You hooked up with Reenzie while we were together; then you told her you wanted to be with me; then when we weren't together, you went right back to her. And look at her. She's sitting there freaked out because she's worried you might still want to be with me."

Sean's raises his blue eyes to look right into mine. "I do," he says, "sometimes."

"Me too," I admit, "pretty much all of the time. But that's not fair. It's not even."

"Hey, kiddies," Reenzie says as she slinks over in her lace-accented black dress and slips her arm through Sean's. "What's up?"

"Got you a soda," Sean says. He shifts his eyes to hers now, and they smile together.

"I'm going to dance," I say. "Come join!"

They don't right away, but eventually they do, and soon we're all out there in a giant knot of my, my mom's, and Erick's friends. Only J.J. doesn't show, but I have high hopes he'll make a dramatic movie entrance as we count down to midnight.

We all pile inside and turn on *Dick Clark's New Year's Rockin' Eve* for the countdown, and scream out the numbers together. After "one," we all shout "HAPPY NEW YEAR!" and throw streamers and blow horns and spin noisemakers, and all the couples fold into each other's arms and kiss and Eddy and Mrs. Rubenstein sing that old New Year's song because they're the only ones who know the words . . .

. . . but no J.J.

I'm disappointed, but I'm not going to let it kill my night. I grab Erick and plant a New Year's kiss on his cheek, then dole them out to Eddy, my mom, Schmidt, and Sugar. Amalita, Taylor, and I corner Jack and all kiss his face at the same time, which he pretends to hate.

I don't kiss Sean, but I hug him. It feels too good. I pull away as soon as I can and meld back into the party.

Ten minutes after midnight, J.J. comes in. He stands in the doorway, craning his neck . . . looking for me? He's wearing a tux, which seems pretty dressed up for a party he's joining so late, but he looks incredible in it.

I run up to him and throw myself into his arms. "J.J.!" I scream. "I'm so glad you're here."

It feels so good when he hugs me back that I start to cry.

"I'm sorry," I say into his jacket. "I'm so, so sorry."

He hugs me a little tighter for just a second, then pulls away. He runs his fingers through his hair. "I can't stay and I can't talk for long because as it is, Carrie's going to kill me for leaving her party."

Proof that I'm the worst human being in the world? After everything I put J.J. through, I flare with jealousy when he mentions Carrie Amernick.

Proof that I have at least a shred of decency? I don't interrupt J.J. and ask if he and Carrie are together now.

"I started to watch the video when you sent it," he says, "but I saw stupid Kyler Leeds and his stupid guitar and I promised myself there was no way I'd ever watch it. But then the year changed and I figured a promise I made last year didn't really matter anymore, and I had already emailed the file to my phone so I'd have it in case I changed my mind. . . ."

"Did you like it?" I ask.

"It kills me to say this because it's Kyler Leeds," he says, "but yeah. I liked it."

"It's everything I wanted to say myself. I just didn't know how."

He nods. "I get it."

He looks uncomfortable. I wish I could help, but I feel like anything I do will just make things worse.

"I miss you," I say. "Can we hang out again?"

He nods again. "Just . . . maybe not like before . . . not for a little while yet."

That makes me want to cry again. J.J.'s tearing up too.

"I have to run," he says. "Tell everyone I said hi. And Happy New Year."

He leans in like he's about to hug me again, but thinks better of it. He turns and jogs back to his car.

"Pay attention, everyone!" Mrs. Rubenstein shouts. "It's my grandson on TV!"

I move toward the screen. It's Kyler, onstage in Times Square. I had no idea he was even going to be on the show. Behind me I hear Taylor, Amalita, and Reenzie whispering about Mrs. Rubenstein and how this is clearly my Kyler connection, but I'm paying attention to the show.

Kyler looks great. He's in full international rock super-star mode. Torn jeans, worn T-shirt that fits him perfectly. He has his guitar slung around his body and speaks into the microphone.

"Happy New Year, everyone! Gonna play a new one for

you tonight. This goes out to a not-so-smooth individual who likes to bump into a certain pop idol fad in the strangest places. If you're watching, I hope your party's going well, and I'd love to see you soon."

I'm totally aware that several pairs of eyes are now staring at me, and several jaws have dropped, but I don't pay attention. I smile, because it sounds to me like I just received an invitation, and I'm pretty sure I can accept and still get back before anyone misses me *too* much.

While the rest of the house listens to Kyler's new song about me and J.J., I run upstairs, lock my bedroom door, and pull out the map. I grab my dry-erase pen and scrawl in big clear letters, right across the green splotch:

Kyler Leeds.

BELLA THORNE

is an actress and an emerging style icon, with over nine million likes on Facebook, six million followers on Twitter, and almost ten million followers on Instagram. Her positive energy, her stay-true-to-yourself message, and her amazing family, plus the love of all the bellarinas/-os around the world, are the driving forces behind everything she does.